Here's what others are saying about *Deadly Gamble*, the first Charlie Parker mystery—

"This is a well-plotted debut mystery with a nice surprise ending and some excellent characterizations. Charlie, in particular, is slick, appealing, and nobody's fool — just what readers want in an amateur sleuth. Look forward to the next installment in what shapes up to be a promising series." — *Booklist*

"Congratulations to both author Shelton and Intrigue Press on this wonderful introduction to both talent centers." — *Book Talk*

"Shelton has created a female sleuth with an original slant to her methods. The mystery itself was in question until the very end. It's a fun and fast read." — *Small Press Review*

"Charlie Parker has a heart as big as all outdoors and it almost spells her finale in *Deadly Gamble*. Connie Shelton's debut mystery offers a down-home view of Albuquerque and a charming new PI." — *Carolyn G. Hart, author of the Death on Demand and Henrie O. mysteries.*

"Very impressed with the professionalism shown in the production of this exciting mystery." — *Books of the Southwest, Tucson, Arizona*

". . . a light, fun read . . . an interesting mix of characters and relationships . . . a cut above most first efforts." — *Bloodhound, The Crime Writer's Connection*

"This is a dandy. Don't miss it!" — *Book Talk*

Vacations Can Be Murder

Connie Shelton

Intrigue Press

For Stephanie

We've laughed together,
Cried together,
Shared life's experiences
in a very special way.

You'll always be my daughter,
I hope you'll always be my friend.

The author wishes to acknowledge the invaluable assistance of the following: Dan Shelton, as always, my technical advisor, plot checker, and moral support; Gretchen Lemons for her last-minute help with proofing; the members of the Moreno Valley Writer's Guild for their continuing encouragement and support; Preston and Grace Myers of Safari Helicopters, Lihue, Kauai, for allowing me to work in their offices and see the helicopter tour industry from the inside; and to the people of Kauai for sharing their lovely island with me for two years of my life. Thanks to all.

Introduction

The writing of this book was begun in early 1992. In September of that year, hurricane Iniki struck the island of Kauai with deadly force. The helicopter industry, along with many others, was devastated. Thirty of the island's thirty-two helicopters suffered major damage. Many of the locations used in this book were obliterated or significantly changed, including the beautiful Westin Hotel which figures so prominently in the story.

Being in the helicopter industry and foreseeing no immediate future for work on Kauai, Dan and I made the decision to relocate back to our native New Mexico.

The writing faltered as I wrestled with the question of whether to portray Kauai as it was when I lived there or to adapt major portions of the story to fit today's situation. Time passed. Kauai began to rebuild. The helicopters were back in business. I completed two more novels and began a third. *Deadly Gamble*, the first in the Charlie Parker series was published. I had to decide what to do with *Vacations*, as it was slated to be the second book in the series.

After much internal wrestling, I decided that I wanted to keep Kauai the way I knew it, and the way I hope it will once again become. As this book goes to press the Westin Kauai has not yet reopened. When it does, I have no idea whether it will be the same as before. Other locations, some real, may or may not return.

Within the helicopter industry, some of the old companies are gone, other new ones have moved in. The Paradise Helicopters in this story was fictitious all along. If a new operator has chosen that name, I have no knowledge of it. I have tried to keep all characters and specific references to the industry purely fictional. New laws have begun to govern helicopter tours over the islands, so the ride today is not precisely as described here, but is spectacular nonetheless.

The people of Kauai and the helicopter operators there have all my best wishes. You will always retain a very special place in my heart.

Connie Shelton
May, 1995

Vacations
Can Be
Murder

1

Vacations mean different things to different people. There's the planning, the packing, the anticipation. Then there's the late arrival, the sunburn, the fuzzy pictures. In my case, add a romance with a good-looking pilot and fourteen stitches in the back of my skull.

I'd chosen Kauai, the northern-most inhabited island in the Hawaiian chain, an egg-shaped dot of land roughly twenty-seven miles wide by thirty-two miles long. Aside from a few atolls, named but unknown to most, it is the first piece of rock east of Japan. No one knows for certain, but somewhere around a thousand years ago, after the volcanoes had quieted down and a life rich with plants and birds had taken over, the Polynesians sailed from the south Pacific, found this tiny grouping of islands, and called them home. A hundred-fifty years ago, white missionary settlers from America arrived to convert these perfectly happy natives from their heathen ways. I don't think we've ever been forgiven for the intrusion. Today, diligent governing keeps mainland-style progress to a minimum. The scent of plumeria and the soft strains of slack-key guitar set a lazy mood. The place is, in mood, climate, and landscape an opposite to my home town Albuquerque.

It was also exactly what I needed after an extremely busy winter and a recent encounter with my former best friend and my ex-fiancé.

I awakened my first morning in the tropics to the sound of surf gently washing at the beach. My room at the Westin Hotel faced Kalapaki Bay and was on the shady side of the building this time of day. The air felt pleasantly cool on my bare skin. I pulled on a light cotton kimono, and stepped out to the lanai. The breeze fluttered my hair, filling my nostrils with the scent of the sea. The bay stretched out before me, the sand on the beach wiped smooth by the night tide.

I wondered what Rusty would think of a romp on the beach. He'd probably be out in the water in no time.

Rusty's an unusual dog of uncertain origins. He's about the build of a Labrador, the color of an Irish setter, and the temperament of a cocker spaniel puppy. I never tell anyone that last part. His size is usually enough to dissuade potential attackers, and he has a way of smiling (no kidding) that shows his teeth, so most people think he's snarling. I usually let them think so.

Rusty adopted me back when I was in college. He started hanging around outside my English Lit class and following me around campus. No matter how many other people fussed over him, he stuck by me. My fiancé had recently eloped with my best friend and I think Rusty sensed my neediness. He has been with me ten years now.

Seven floors below me the ocean looked like a rippled piece of azurite with short ruffs of white lace at the edges. There was a time-delay effect as I watched the lapping waves roll onto the beach several seconds before their soft whooshing sound reached my ears. The sweet smell of tropical flowers rose toward me, borne on the humid air. Distance miniaturized the mosaic-patterned stone walkway below, and I watched two men in hotel uniform pull their golf carts together side by side. A cigarette changed hands, and their laughter drifted up to me. They lounged, obviously in no hurry to rush back to work.

I took a deep breath and stretched, enjoying the tiny shot of adrenalin to my extremities. It felt good to be away from the routine, to have my taxes done, and Ron back at the office handling things there again.

In real life I'm a CPA. I'm also partners with my brother, Ron, in a small private investigation firm. Ron is the PI; I'm just supposed to keep the finances running right. This past winter, though, Ron broke his leg in a skiing accident, leaving me to run the whole show for a couple of months.

By the first of May I decided I was entitled to a break. I was glad, for a change, not to be responsible.

The beach below was absolutely deserted; the flat gray expanse of sand looked cool, as nearly colorless as the pale sky beyond. Catamarans and small sailboats, their sails neatly rolled, lined the fringe between sand and grass safely beyond the tide's reach. The beach towel concession stand was securely shuttered. It must be early. I glanced at my watch. Six o'clock. Ten, Albuquerque time. No wonder I felt so wide awake.

The empty beach looked tempting, but the sun hadn't reached it yet. The air would probably be a bit nippy to bare skin that had been swaddled in protective woolens the past five months. Another whiff of a breeze shook the palm fronds and raised tiny bumps on my skin. My stomach spoke, reminding me that my last meal had been on an airplane, so long ago that I had trouble calculating the hours. Breakfast seemed to be in order.

Two hours later, after a shower and a mushroom omelet, I felt ready to get out and explore. Like any diligent tourist, I had picked up an assortment of maps and guidebooks at the airport, so I decided to find out what this paradise had to offer. I jammed my bikini, a towel, and a bottle of sun screen into my canvas tote, made sure I had my wallet and keys to the rental car, and left the room.

Last night my arrival had been late and I hadn't compre-hended the full magnificence of the Westin Hotel and its grounds. Walking out now, I passed through the elegant lower lobby with its thick blue and gold Oriental rug, teak registra-tion desk and Chinese antiques. One wall opened to reveal an open courtyard about the size of a city block. A tiled pond filled most of it. In its center, marble horses reared dramatically amidst splashing fountains. Live swans dipped their graceful necks into the water, coming up periodically for air. Tropical birds in shades of turquoise, green, red and yellow sat on perches around the perimeter of the pond, squawking and tossing peanut shells onto the floor.

From this lower lobby, a long escalator crawled upward to another lobby. Open to the outside, where cars circled under the porte-cochere, the upper lobby bustled with activity. Bell-men unloaded bags from the backs of taxis and limousines, while dazed-looking sweaty tourists emerged with their too-warm clothing pasted to their backs.

A diorama of the Westin complex sat stop a large table, covered with a plexiglass dome. I studied it for a moment before heading to the parking lot.

My red Sunbird convertible was right where I'd left it — I thought. Actually, there were six of them in that row, and four in the next. I glanced around to see whether anyone was about to witness my embarrassment as I tried my key until I found the right one.

Luckily, it worked on the second try. Just to verify, I pulled the rental receipt from the glove compartment to be sure my name was on it. My face flushed as I remembered how cool I thought I'd be driving a convertible around Hawaii. Apparently, several hundred other tourists had the same idea.

The sky was clear, as blue as a Wedgwood candy dish. I could feel the humidity, but the early morning air was cool enough to keep it from becoming oppressive. I put the top down and stowed my beach gear behind the front seat. I had decided during breakfast to take a drive up the main highway to see where it would lead me.

I studied my map as the car warmed up. The main town, Lihue, is situated at approximately the four-o'clock position on this almost-round bit of land. From Lihue the road goes north where it dead-ends slightly beyond the twelve-o'clock spot, or south, curving upward to the west, and ending around nine-o'clock. The remaining fourth of the coastline and much of the mountainous interior are inaccessible by car. Getting my bearings, I decided to head toward town first.

The tree-shaded Westin driveway took me out toward Rice Street. Plantings of philodendron alternated with bright clumps of white, purple, pink, and coral impatiens. White stone urns, decorated with garlands of stone flowers, stood in well-planned alcoves. I turned right onto Rice Street, driving up a hill, the cutaway side of which was raw-looking red earth, the color of rust. I had no trouble finding the sign that directed me toward Highway 56.

At Ahukini Road, which led back to the Lihue airport, I took advantage of the red light to consult my map again. The overhead whopp-whopp of a helicopter's rotor blades grabbed my attention. The aircraft came straight toward me, then made a graceful turn almost over my head. It swung in an arc, dipping lower, disappearing behind a tall field of sugar cane. My interest quickened immediately.

I have always loved flying. Living in Albuquerque, I'd had no trouble bumming hot air balloon rides on several occasions. The sensation of floating soundlessly above the earth is like no other. I'd even tried an ultralight once. I draw the line at hang gliding but as long as it has a power source, I'm game.

An impatient horn tooted behind me, jerking me back to the present. I drove through the intersection, and pulled to the side as soon as I could safely do so.

Another helicopter lifted off, just the other side of the cane field on my right. It looked like a giant dragonfly as it paused for a couple of seconds then made a wide circle around the airport tower and headed for the low hills behind me. It soon became just a dot in the sky.

I flipped open the guidebook. Paradise Helicopters. The ad lay right there, under my index finger. *Fly Through Paradise With Us*, it announced.

The color photo showed a helicopter poised before the white streamer of a long waterfall. The advertising blurb promised the ride of a lifetime, a chance to view the hidden mysteries of Kauai in a way no one else could offer. They claimed the most experienced pilots, a perfect safety record, and discount coupons for restaurant dinners if you booked direct.

Well, who could pass up all that?

A quick study of the map told me that their offices were right here in Lihue, just a couple of blocks away. I watched for an open spot in the traffic, and hung a U. Paradise Helicopters was in a small strip shopping center, tucked between a pizza parlor and an aloha wear shop. Trees fashioned out of bougainvillea vines dotted the parking lot at intervals. I pulled the Sunbird into an open space in front of the glass-fronted offices, right beside an identical red car.

Smugly, I remembered to memorize my plate number before I went inside.

The air-conditioned office was a pleasant contrast to the hot sun outside. The front lobby was designed to be as comfy as a living room. Rattan furniture, with tropical print cushions in pale shades of blue, yellow, and gray, was placed in a homey grouping facing a TV set. The TV was off now, but I could see it was connected to a VCR. A selection of tapes was stacked next to it, featuring titles such as "Kauai By Air" and "Your Flight of Memories."

The warm-up, I supposed, where the passengers could sit around before their flights, viewing the spectacles yet to come, and trying not to think about being too nervous.

Colorful helicopter posters decorated the walls and the air smelled faintly of flowers. An elaborate arrangement of bright red and yellow heliconia and puffy gray protea stood almost five feet tall in one corner. A tiny model helicopter hung suspended above the flowers by an invisible nylon line.

"Hi there!" A bubbly voice greeted me like I was a long lost friend from the past. I glanced around and saw that the front office was deserted except for the bubbler, a young woman seated at a desk near the back. She was so petite and tan that she made me feel like the great white whale with my hundred-twenty pounds of winter pale flesh.

Her fluffy wheat-colored hair was pulled up on top with a stretchy hot-pink band, from which it spewed like a wild tuft of pampas grass. She wore an elaborate combination of shimmering pink and blue eye shadow and had probably used close to a whole tube of mascara. Too bad, because she was too pretty, and definitely too young, for the drastically overdone look. She had a plastic badge pinned over her left breast that told me her name was Melanie.

"You wanna take the flight?" Twin dimples sculpted themselves into her tan cheeks.

"Yeah, do you have anything available today?" I stepped up to the teak counter which divided her desk off from the rest of the room.

She lifted the top sheet of a stack of pages which were held together at the top with two large bulldog clips. Her eyes scanned the second page, while her perfectly aligned teeth worked at masticating her pencil eraser. Her orthodontist would not be happy to see that.

"I have a single open at three o'clock."

"Nothing sooner?" Once I make up my mind to do something, I want to do it *now*.

"Not for a single. Now, if you were a couple . . . But, see, singles are harder to find, and I have to make it come out even, and there's this couple with a kid at three . . ."

I could see this was going to lead to a long explanation which wasn't making much sense anyway.

"That's okay." I held one palm out toward her. "I'll take the three o'clock."

I could tell by the way the dimples reappeared that I had alleviated some kind of huge concern in the back of her tiny little mind. She sat in her swivel chair, one leg tucked up under her, prepared to take my vital statistics.

"Great! Great, now I need your name and your weight."

I told her.

"Charlie? Isn't that kind of a funny name for a girl?"

I felt my eyes begin to roll. I was in no mood to explain that I had been named after my mother's two maiden aunts. Charlotte Louise Parker had been a hell of a name to stick a tiny baby with, but I was a little young at the time to have a vote in the matter. Growing up with two older brothers had turned me into a tough little tomboy, and Charlie was the name that stuck.

Melanie seemed to sense that maybe I didn't owe her an explanation so she busied herself with taking an imprint of my credit card. I watched her fill in the rest of the information in over-emphasized round letters with lots of extra curls attached.

"Would you like to see where the tour will take you?" she asked, once business was taken care of.

I figured the big map on the wall with a path outlined in fluorescent red dots pretty well told the story, but she wanted to be helpful. She seemed determined, so I didn't object when she came around the end of the counter. Her pink Spandex shorts and cut-off top made me realize once again that I'd put on a few pounds over the winter. Her ensemble didn't exactly strike me as proper office attire; obviously they do everything a bit more casually here in Hawaii.

She had just launched into a recital of all the unpronounceable Hawaiian places I'd see, when a man appeared from a back office.

He wore a navy blue knit shirt with the Paradise logo in white on the left side of his chest and a pair of navy twill shorts. His wavy brown hair was generously scattered with gray. His eyes drooped slightly at the outer corners, and there was a deep worry-crease between the dark brows. He was slim and stood with an erectness in his posture that suggested a military career. I noticed his watch. It was gold with all sorts of extra dials on the face. He wore a heavy gold ring on his right hand, none on the left.

"Mack!" my exuberant little hostess exclaimed. She turned to introduce us. "Charlie, this is Mack Garvey, the owner of Paradise Helicopters. He only flies on weekdays, so today you'll be flying with our other pilot, Drake Langston."

I held out my hand to Mack. He shot a quick flicker of a smile my way as he shook it, but I could tell his mind was elsewhere. He scowled toward Melanie's Spandex-clad behind. He opened his mouth like he wanted to say something, then closed it again. It seemed like a good time for me to go.

"Nice meeting you, Mack," I said, heading toward the door.

He grunted a distracted "You, too," as he crossed behind the desk to check the flight manifest.

Melanie piped up: "Bye, Charlie! Come back at two-thirty to check in for your flight." She waved and grinned, like we were best pals who planned to meet in the high school cafeteria at lunch time.

With a few hours to kill, I decided to explore the nearby countryside. Driving west out of Lihue took me inland. According to my guidebook, there was an old plantation house, now open to the public, along this road. Apparently, sugar is still big business here, although the romance of the plantation days was over long ago.

Now, large corporations own all the sugar plantations. The work has become mechanized. Long gone are the hundreds of immigrant laborers working in the fields cutting the tough cane. Their descendants have gone on to pursue other ventures — Chinese, Japanese, Korean, Filipino and Portuguese — all blending into a unique society of their own. I made a right turn and joined the line of traffic heading away from town.

A shopping center and several fast food places passed on my left. I wondered if Taco Bell in Hawaii tasted the same as ours in New Mexico.

The historic house soon appeared on the right. I turned in at the paved drive, between massive lava stone pillars. The Tudor style mansion sat well back from the road. It was trimmed with stone accents, and had about a half acre of dark brown shingle roof. I followed the snaking driveway to a discreet parking lot at the side.

Behind the main house, I could see stables and groupings of small wooden houses. Acres of lawn spread in all directions, as perfect as a carpet. Bright tropical flowers bloomed in clumps surrounding the outbuildings.

A small white gazebo stood in the shade of a banyan tree. White chairs, decorated with pink ribbons and flowers, indicated that a wedding would take place later. Two gardeners with hedge clippers snipped at a hibiscus bush and I wondered how many workers it took to run a house this size.

A bored-looking Clydesdale, hitched to an old-fashioned carriage, stood near the front entrance. A young man wearing a blousy white shirt, brown knee britches, and a pasted-on smile stood near the horse's head, waving to passers-by and attempting to drum up business for his carriage rides at seven dollars a pop.

Inside the main house the foyer was cool and shady. I picked up a brochure showing the floor plan.

The house had apparently been built in the 1930s by one of the second generation sugar families. The spacious living and dining rooms were furnished as they had been at the time. The covered outdoor lanai was now a restaurant, serving in "casual elegance" beginning at eleven.

I made my way up the heavy wooden staircase with its thick handrail, curious to see what a real "morning room" looked like. Immediately, I was disappointed to see that all the upstairs rooms had been converted to shops. I had hoped to see at least a couple of them decorated authentically as bedrooms and whatever else their original purposes had been.

Jewelry, silk clothing and art prints filled the spaces, obscuring both the views from the windows and the rooms' original ambiance. I meandered through the halls for a few minutes, but soon lost interest. I could have just as well gone to the mall.

Downstairs, brightly colored posters caught my eye in a little shop stuck in a corner that carried books and art prints. Perhaps my neighbor, Elsa Higgins, would enjoy a book on the aloha state. Since she was minding Rusty for me this week I wanted to take her something.

The woman behind the desk put down the book she was reading when I walked in. She wore a flowing gauzy creation of tie dyed cotton. Her face was clear of makeup, and there was a gentle web of wrinkles at the corners of her eyes. Her light brown waist-length hair showed ribbons of gray. She wore it pulled back from her face with tortoise colored plastic combs. Two fresh plumeria flowers were tucked behind one ear. If this were still the sixties, I'm sure she would have flashed me a peace sign.

She let me browse the shelves for a few minutes before speaking. I found a picture book I thought Mrs. Higgins might like.

"Are you enjoying your stay on the island?" she asked as I approached her desk. Her voice was low and soothing, like she might be accomplished at leading meditation sessions.

"So far, I am. It's only my first day here." I ran my fingers through a stack of bookmarks on display. They were made of dried flowers pressed between plastic to form tiny bouquets. "I'm taking a helicopter ride later to get a better view of the whole place. Paradise Helicopters. Have you heard of them?"

"Oh, yes." Something in her face shut down, and her voice took on a very un-soothing edge.

"What's the matter?" Visions of a bad safety record popped into my head.

She fiddled with a basket of postcard-sized art prints near the register, rearranging and aligning them. I stood, waiting, not intending to let her out of the question. Finally, she looked back up at me. Her answer was not at all what I expected.

"The state has let this helicopter tour thing get way out of hand," she said abruptly. "Those horrid noise polluters have no business flying over the pristine beauty of this land. It's a travesty, what they're doing to the land. The state won't control them, and as a result, they'll end up destroying what we have here."

2

The gentle gray eyes had taken on a hard edge and the vehemence in her voice startled me. I couldn't imagine how a few helicopters flying around the island would destroy the land, but clearly I'd walked right into a nest of local political debate here. I had no intention, however, of staying in it, especially not on my vacation.

She looked like she was just warming up, though, as she reached to take the book I had picked out. I set the book on the desk, murmured a polite thanks, and turned toward the door.

No matter where you go, you can find these battling factions, each righteously expounding their beliefs. I've found that there are two sides to every story, and I wasn't about to get dragged into this one.

Outside, I took a deep breath. I felt like such a chicken. I wasn't raised to duck out on a debate. My father would have politely let the woman go on. My mother would have joined in the fight, taking a side, any side. But, I just didn't have the heart for it. I was glad to be out of there. A brisk walk around the perimeter of the old plantation house helped dissipate my frustration and I glanced briefly at some of the outbuildings before returning to my car.

I found a touristy restaurant in town that served an excellent grilled chicken sandwich and tangy fresh pineapple for lunch. My open-air table faced the bay and I breathed deeply, letting the sea air wash away the last remnants of the shop woman's negativeness. I took my time over lunch and arrived at Paradise Helicopters' office precisely on time.

Melanie greeted me again by name in her almost too-friendly way.

The other passengers had already arrived, a husband and wife with a kid about four years old. He was a handful, whining and tugging at his mother in that center-of-attention way that most preschoolers seem to have. They introduced themselves as the Johnsons — Joe, Brenda and young Cory.

"It'll be a few minutes until the shuttle driver gets back," Melanie explained. "Why don't you put a video on, Charlie?"

Her hands were busy filling out Joe Johnson's credit card slip, but her eyes were riveted on young Cory, whose gaze was fixated on the model helicopter that hung above the now-endangered flower arrangement in the corner. He was raising one foot, apparently ready to use the large vase as a step stool.

I took Melanie's cue. "Here, Cory, let's see what this one's about."

I grabbed a tape that looked like a cartoon and stuffed it into the machine. The deedly-deedly music attracted his attention only seconds before two heliconia stalks would have met a nasty fate.

Brenda sat on the sofa, flipping through a magazine, oblivious to her son's actions.

I turned my attention to the scenery outside.

Twenty minutes later, my fellow passengers and I were on our way to the heliport in Paradise's company van. Sugar cane grew eight feet tall along Ahukini Road, acre after acre of thin green blades. In the distance it stretched on, like a giant's unmown lawn. We went through the intersection where I'd sat only this morning watching the helicopters come and go; now we headed toward the airport.

The van driver veered left, away from the main terminal building, past a collection of smaller general aviation hangars. On our left, a row of helicopter pads was laid out and numbered, like the squares on a huge board game. A couple of the pads contained parked helicopters with their rotor blades tied down.

For the most part, though, the place was a regular beehive. I watched two helicopters land, and three more take off, just in the time it took our driver to park and unload us from the van. Small as the aircraft were, each had its own distinctive paint scheme.

A chain link fence, eight feet high topped with a double strand of rusty barbed wire, separated the pads from the parking area. We were instructed to wait behind it until our driver signaled. Meanwhile, the blue and tan JetRanger we would ride in hovered a short distance away, apparently waiting for another, in line ahead of it, to make its landing.

My attention was drawn to the other one as it landed. The pilot brought it in fast and landed with a bump. Before his shuttle driver could get there, the pilot had opened his door and stepped down. It didn't seem a very safe practice to me, leaving the machine running with passengers inside and no pilot.

The pilot motioned toward his driver, calling him over. He stood leaning over the young kid, shaking a finger in his face. I couldn't catch the words, but his body language was easily understood. The young driver cowered at the onslaught, and the passengers inside looked uncomfortable.

A tug at my sleeve got my attention. Paradise's helicopter had landed, and the previous passengers were out and waiting near the van. I followed our shuttle driver, and stood back as he opened my door for me. The tremendous whirl from the rotor blades caught at the edges of my shorts, whipping the fabric against my legs. Luckily, I hadn't worn a skirt. I stepped up, and slid into my seat. The pilot helped me find my seat belt.

I had been given the front seat next to him, while the Johnson family were lined up across the rear. I was thankful that the noise of the engine and rotor blades forced us all to wear headsets. If I'd had to listen to one more plaintive demand from Cory in the back seat I'd have decked him.

The twenty minute wait in the office before heading to the airport had just about cinched my decision not to have children. This one was a whiner, and Joe and Brenda Johnson apparently didn't believe in suppressing their child's natural outspokenness.

I caught our pilot's glance at the kid as they were loading, and we exchanged a brief raised eyebrow. He helped me put my headset on while the shuttle driver assisted those in the back seats.

"Can you hear me all right?" His voice was low and soft, coming into my right ear piece. I nodded.

"I'm Drake Langston," he introduced himself.

"Charlie Parker," I said, extending my hand, "and no, I'm not the jazz musician."

He laughed, a low and pleasant chuckle.

"No, I would have never mistaken the two of you," he said. "Charlie — I like that."

There was something in the smile he flashed at me that I found immensely attractive. Not to mention the touch of gray in his dark hair and the sureness with which he handled the controls.

The muscles of his forearms rippled slightly as he flipped a couple of switches. He wore a navy knit shirt with the company logo on the chest, like Mack had worn earlier in the day. His khaki slacks were neatly creased. I absorbed all this in less than a minute before my attention strayed again to the other helipad where the angry pilot was still shaking his finger in the other guy's face.

He had pulled his headset off now, and the wind whipped his red ball cap off. That provoked his anger all over again, and he ordered his driver to retrieve it. He stomped back to his aircraft, jerking the door open.

"I'm sorry you saw that," Drake interrupted. "His name is Bill Steiner. That guy is trouble all the way around. Gives a bad name to the rest of us."

"What's he so upset about?"

"Who knows? With him it could be anything. He just better hope there's not an FAA man out here right now. He'd be busted for sure, leaving his passengers like that."

I wondered what makes some people need to flaunt this kind of behavior in public. Perhaps they like the feeling of control over others that it gives them. Behavior like that does have a certain show-stopping effect.

Meanwhile, the rest of our group were buckled into their seats, and the doors securely latched. With Mr. and Mrs. Doormat and young Rowdy settled into the back seats, Drake began a safety briefing. Cory promptly stuck his hand out the narrow vent window the minute Drake mentioned this as a safety no-no. He flashed Brenda Johnson a glare, and she grabbed her kid's hands. Her eyes bored into the back of Drake's head with a look I once saw on a female German shepherd with eight pups.

Drake had switched radio frequencies, and I watched his

lips move as he cleared us for takeoff with the tower. The turbine engine whined and the ground retreated as the craft rose straight up before it picked up gentle forward momentum.

It was fascinating to watch Drake fly the machine. Both feet and both hands worked, each doing something different. I envied his coordination and admired the aircraft's maneuverability. I watched as the airport fell away at our feet, becoming miniaturized in just a couple of minutes.

Drake pointed out the sprawling Westin complex with its golf course, half-dozen restaurants, and labyrinth of canals as we passed over. Nawiliwili Harbor lay below, with tiny boats moored in slips and a large freight barge off-loading orange and brown containers. Beyond the harbor, Drake indicated the Menehune Fish Pond.

Apparently, the menehune are the Hawaiian equivalent of leprechauns, performing mystical feats in the middle of the night. In this case, they had supposedly carried lava rocks down from the mountains to dam up a section of river, forming a pond. The wall looked about three hundred yards long. The little guys really had a busy night of it. And, for this they were paid one shrimp each. Talk about minimum wage.

"The primary crop on the island is sugar cane," Drake's steady voice informed us. "We also commercially grow coffee and macadamia nuts, which you see in the fields below us now."

In the back seat, the missus attempted resignedly to keep control over her rambunctious offspring while her oblivious husband snapped pictures from his window seat.

I turned my attention back to the scenery. We were approaching mountainous country, and I could see that Drake was about to maneuver us in front of a triple deck frothy white waterfall.

"Where's your camera?" he asked me. Again, that smile, and the voice like velvet.

"I'm not much of a photographer," I answered. In truth, I didn't want to miss out on the panoramic view by looking through an undersized view finder.

He took us to two or three more waterfalls — I was beginning to lose count — then headed toward Waimea Canyon. I loved the way it felt like the bottom dropped out as we flew over the edge.

Waimea Canyon was a mini version of the Grand Canyon, amazingly un-tropical. The red earth was dry here, and I even spotted clusters of cactus growing on some of the ridges. We flew past a lookout point where tiny tourists stood by a railing, looking up at us and pointing.

Shortly after flying through the canyon, we broke out over the tops of the razor sharp ridges of the Na Pali coast. The contrast was remarkable. The multi-colored earth stratified throughout the canyon had been softly muted by time and the river's flow.

The sharp peaks of the Na Pali, on the other hand, spoke of indomitable strength as they'd withstood brutal attacks by the wind and sea for thousands upon thousands of years. I realized the pictures don't come close to doing this place justice.

Twice, I caught myself staring open-mouthed as we skirted the sharp peaks which dropped straight down into the sea, each hiding a tiny secluded beach in its shadow. The scene repeated itself again and again down the distant shore.

Drake had planned the stereo music playing through our headsets to correspond with the terrain. Soft and gentle at first, quick and exciting over the rugged parts.

"Folks, normally we try to fly into the Kalalau Valley, but it's become socked in with clouds the last hour or so," Drake's voice came through, still confident and clear. "I'll take us a little way farther up the coast to Hanakapiai, and we can buzz in there for a close-up."

None of us knew one valley from another, anyway. It sounded fine to me. It was all beautiful.

The back seat group wasn't saying anything at this point. Cory was pulling the airsick bags out of their wrappers, while Brenda ignored him, grabbing a moment of silence for herself. Drake glanced back at them, and we exchanged another raised eyebrow.

We did a few more circles and turns over the small beaches. The sand was the color of a freshly baked sugar cookie with turquoise water lapping gently at the edges of it. We headed inland up a narrow valley with high lava peaks on either side of us.

"As early as 800 A.D., the ancient Polynesians had sailed across open ocean to discover these islands, and many of them settled in these very . . . valleys." Drake's voice broke off quietly, and I turned to look at him.

"What is it?" I tried to speak loud enough for him to catch my words, but he wasn't looking at me, and couldn't hear me over the engine noise.

His face had turned pale under his tan. I followed his line of sight down to the rugged lava embankment below.

A very dead-looking man lay sprawled across the rocks.

Except for his bright red shirt with geometric patterns of blue and gold, he would have been difficult to spot. His dark slacks and shoes blended with the lava rocks and I didn't see any flashy jewelry. He appeared to be about five-ten, slim, dark haired.

I looked back up at Drake, then glanced again at the back seat. They were all occupied, Cory with a pile of shredded paper and plastic now at his feet, and the parents, staring up at the rugged cliffs surrounding us.

Drake had switched radio frequencies again and was

speaking rapidly, although those of us in the aircraft could no longer hear him.

I stared out again at the dead man, noticing details out of habit. He was about a hundred yards in from the shore, lying face down in an area where the terrain started to rise, the lava rocks becoming rougher farther inland. I wondered how he had gotten there.

Drake had mentioned one narrow foot trail along the coast, which hikers and campers used. Had the man gotten off the trail and fallen? It would be easy to do out here. The endless rows of sharp ridges looked impossible.

Yet the picture struck me as not quite plausible. For one thing, he didn't have a backpack or any other gear that I could see. And his clothes weren't right. The multi-colored shirt looked silky, more like a dress shirt than outdoor wear. And the shoes. Black dress shoes. No one in his right mind would attempt to hike in those.

Who was this out-of-place victim?

Drake had circled as casually as possible, and we headed now out of the narrow confines of the valley.

"What's happening?" I mouthed.

He reached forward to the center console, and flipped a toggle switch. I noticed that the top position was labeled "Passengers", while the bottom position said "Co-Pilot." He switched it down. Now the back seat group could not hear him.

"I radioed what I saw," he told me. The office is rescheduling my next flight, and the airport people want me to bring the police out. Operating as we do here, on aloha time, I'll probably be tied up with this until late tonight." His face had taken on lines I hadn't seen earlier. He suddenly looked drained.

He toggled up the intercom switch so all could hear and swung the helicopter around the end of the sharp rocky ridge. Beyond, the land opened up again into a wide valley where taro fields shone in emerald squares below. Drake mechanically recited the names of the towns below and the famous people who inhabited the large estates that bordered a golf course and lined the beaches.

The music flowing into our headsets turned into a haunting Hawaiian song, whose words were unfamiliar but whose melody cried with pain.

The helicopter entered the island's main volcanic crater through a broken-out V in its side, a place where lava flowed into the valley below in ancient times. On three sides, narrow waterfalls cascaded down the shiny black rock. Above us, the top of the mountain was shrouded in dark gray clouds, heavy with moisture, that misted down onto our windshield. The aircraft seemed tiny and insignificant in the huge cavern-like space. The music drummed heavily. The whole effect was melancholy gray.

Once outside the gloomy crater, again the sun shone and we finished making our circle tour of the island. Somehow, though, I had the impression Drake was rushing through it, his mind still back there in the Hanakapiai Valley. Truthfully, I didn't hear much of the tour myself. My mind began to mull over the possibilities.

Drake brought the helicopter in over the heliport, cruised slowly down the flight line, and set it softly down on the pad. While the waiting shuttle driver assisted the others from the back seat, I fished around in my purse.

"Drake, if you can use help with this, give me a call," I said, handing him my business card. "I'm staying at the Westin."

"RJP Investigations?"

"I'm a partner in a PI firm back home," I explained. "And from the look of it, I'd say this is no simple hiking accident. Looks to me like a murder."

I unbuckled my seat belt, and stepped down to the tarmac. I glanced back once. Drake was sitting motionless, holding my card in his hand. I didn't know whether he'd call or not, but I did know that my natural curiosity wasn't going to let go of this. Now that I'd voiced it aloud — the M word — I'd have to find out what had happened.

So much for my vacation.

3

I got into private investigating, very indirectly, because I took an accounting course in college. I was twenty years old when I realized that I was about to come into a fairly decent inheritance, and I had never even balanced a checkbook. It was my second year of college, my second year of foundering around with no clear goal in mind.

My parents had died in a plane crash when I was sixteen, leaving money in a trust fund for me, to be collected when I turned twenty-one. With this momentous occasion near at hand, I decided I'd better become fiscally responsible. My brother, Ron, talked me into the accounting course.

Whether I really had a talent for the subject, or whether it was pure luck that I got professor Rosa Alvarez for the class, I'm not sure. She definitely helped ease my way through basic accounting with her genuine affinity for both her subject and her students. It's one thing to know a subject, another to teach it. Professor Alvarez had that rare ability to assess a student's learning mode, and fit the subject to it.

Under her guidance, the basic stuff about debits and credits came easily to me, and I could soon balance my checkbook with one hand tied behind my back. In fact, I found that I really liked working with numbers. You could add and subtract them, multiply and divide them, play with them, and in the end, you balanced them. I liked that. It pleased my tidy side.

I finished all the courses, and took the CPA exam. I joined one of Albuquerque's largest and most prestigious accounting firms, and was soon on my way up the corporate ladder.

The problem was, I hated it — the corporate part. I hated putting on the pin-striped suit every day and playing the little business games. I detested the office politics, including the whispered gatherings around the coffee maker and the larger-than-life dramatic battles for new clients and prized promotions. It just wasn't *me*.

What on earth does this have to do with my becoming an investigator? Well, I *said* it was indirect. With a couple of years accounting experience under my belt, the Fortune 500 might not have been ready for me yet, but I was pretty sharp with an average balance sheet.

It was about this time I sensed a certain amount of edginess in our old trusted family lawyer whenever I got too specific about my inheritance money. Well, I don't have to spell it out.

It took some digging on my part, including one (probably illegal) foray into his file cabinets before I could prove what I suspected, but in the end I managed to extricate myself and what was left of my money from the dirty rat.

The education had not come cheaply. He had siphoned off over fifty thousand dollars, but I learned a lot from that caper. One, a lawyer operating just within the fringes of the law usually knows what he's doing and is, therefore, difficult to catch. And two, it's not that hard to pick the lock on a filing cabinet.

The lawyer was never prosecuted for his deeds, but somehow word got around about his secret foreign bank account and almost overnight a lot of his rich, conservative clients dropped him. Funny how those things sometimes happen.

Several months later my neighbor, Elsa Higgins, became concerned that her insurance agent was acting a bit secretively toward her. I offered to check it out. She was pleased to learn that her quarterly annuity checks were suddenly going to be twice as large, while her agent went to have a little chat with the state insurance commission. Elsa sent her good friend, Edna Walsh to see me, and . . .

Two years later, my brother, Ron, was down and out after his divorce. Bernadette had taken the kids and had really soaked him financially. Even though New Mexico is a community property state, if one party is greedy enough and the other is easy-going enough, the law ain't worth diddly.

Ron came out of it with his clothes, his car, and the oldest cast-offs of their furniture. He needed a break, so I helped him set up a little agency. I quit the accounting firm, and Ron and I became partners.

We started out with him as the investigator and me as the financial person, but gradually I've become more and more involved. Ron handled people's dirty little personal secrets, and I took the financial ones. Well, the cases started to get more serious as time went by, but I still enjoy sniffing out fraud the best. They say murder, like greatness, is sometimes thrust upon us.

I left the heliport feeling rather stirred up, like someone had taken a wire whisk to my insides. The exhilaration of the ride, combined with the sight of the body, and the inevitable hundreds of unanswered questions whirred around in my head. The memory of Drake Langston's smile flickered through my mental banks like a subliminal message, too.

The heavy clouds threatening the north shore had not moved to this side yet. The afternoon still felt early, so I went back to my hotel, deciding to grab a little sun time.

The beach wasn't crowded at all, as I tossed my towel out on the sand. The warm humid air gave my bikini-clad skin a soft caress. The sun felt good on my winter-pale limbs, and I had the latest Tom Clancy novel to keep me company. I read the words, but didn't absorb much. My mind wouldn't let go of the afternoon.

The unanswered questions about the body on the rocks wouldn't leave me alone. I pictured Drake flying back out to the spot with the police.

Who was the dead man? I wondered if he had identification on him.

And, how on earth did he end up in such a remote spot?

Kalapaki Bay gleamed silver in the afternoon sun, winking at me, mocking my questions. In the distance, a barge piled high with containers chugged slowly toward an unseen pier. Two catamarans, whose rainbow-colored sails puffed outward, criss-crossed the bay, steering clear of the dozen or so boogie boarders paddling near shore. A young couple strolled slowly, their arms wound around each other's waists. Three boys, eightish, tossed a plastic saucer among themselves. I watched without really absorbing.

Was the dead man a tourist? A local? Could his death possibly have been an accident? The questions continued to buzz around inside me.

Twenty minutes was about all I could manage on the beach before I had to start moving. The brilliant sun and the troublesome thoughts pounding at my head were getting to me. It really was none of my business, I told myself several times. I hadn't been asked to get involved.

On the other hand, it's not in my nature to just sit. I slipped a cotton cover-up on over my bikini, stepped into sandals, and gathered my junk into a canvas tote. So far I'd seen but a fraction of the Westin's sprawling complex. I could amuse myself by wandering through the shops before going upstairs to change for dinner.

I followed the mosaic-patterned walkway that I'd observed from my lanai this morning, skirted the huge freeform swimming pool, and sought out the shady shopping arcade.

I wasn't sure I'd ever seen a more glittering hundred yards of shopping anywhere in my life. Certainly not in Albuquerque.

Here, under one long colonnade resided the Who's Who of fashion and fripperies. I helped myself to a generous spritz of Giorgio at one perfume counter before I realized that I would soon be showering it off anyway.

A white sweater caught my eye at another shop across the way, and I drifted toward it. It was an unsubstantial bit of fluff, like a dandelion going to seed, with a spill of gold sequins falling over the left shoulder.

Normally, I'm a jeans and t-shirt kind of person. But I can dress up on occasion — when I really have to. Decked out in sequins and satin shoes, I can manage quite nicely at a country club soirée or a night at the opera.

I reached out to give the sweater a stroke, when something else in the shop caught my eye. A red silk shirt with a pattern of blue and gold.

A shirt I would never forget.

"Beautiful sweater, isn't it?" The shop girl startled me. Standing right beside her the whole time, I had mistaken her for a mannequin.

She did have a mannequin sort of body, straight and slim. And her makeup was magazine perfect. Either she was Oriental, or her dark hair cut blunt at chin length and straight across the bangs gave that appearance. My eyes registered all this in less than a second, then riveted back to the red shirt.

My feet carried me toward the shirt without my brain even telling them to. I reached out toward it.

Silk.

Expensive.

"These are very nice." The mannequin was right at my side, touching the multi-colored shirt. "We've only had them a couple of days. An exclusive from a New York manufacturer. We're the only shop on the island carrying them."

"Really." I felt my interest quickening. "Have you sold many yet?"

"I sold two yesterday," she answered. Her long tapered fingers flipped through the hangers on the rack, counting. "I guess that's all. The evening girl must not have sold any."

"Do you remember selling one to a slim, dark haired man?"

She began to look uncomfortable with the questions. Discretion is a job requirement in major hotels, and she looked worried that she might have already said too much.

"I'm with an investigation firm." I pulled my wallet from my tote bag, and handed her my business card. I hoped she wasn't going to question that I was from out of state.

Apparently not, because she loosened up considerably.

"Yes," she said, "there was such a man here yesterday morning. He and his lady friend bought several items. He chose the red shirt for himself, and she took a new bathing suit, a skimpy bikini with a matching cover-up jacket. Neon green."

"You have quite a memory."

I could almost see a faint blush under the pale matte makeup.

"Well, it's been slow recently. We don't get that much traffic through the shops. And they were such a striking pair."

"How so?"

She chewed at the inside of her cheek for a second, deciding just how indiscreet she should be.

"Well, he was well-groomed, but somehow it had a false ring to it. You know, the hair fluffed and sprayed, the teeth capped, the nails manicured." She glanced around to confirm that we were still alone. "Like a game show host."

I got the picture. "And the girl?"

"She hung on him like they were honeymooners, and yet that didn't seem quite right, either. I see lots of honeymooners in here. These two weren't madly in love."

Madly in lust was more like it, I guessed.

"One other question. Did you happen to get his name?"

"She called him 'baby' the whole time they were in the shop. He called her Susan." She chewed at her cheek a little more. "Let me think — he used a credit card. I believe yesterday's slips are still here. The manager from the main store hasn't come by to get them yet."

I followed her to the cash register, mentally crossing my fingers that I'd get something informative.

She reached below the counter, and pulled out a large brown envelope. Carefully bending up the metal brads, she extracted a smaller white envelope. She pulled out a small stack of credit card slips, and flipped through them.

"Here it is. Gilbert Page." She held the slip out to me. He'd spent over six hundred dollars.

"Do you know if he's registered here at the hotel?"

"I assume so. Most of our customers are. Although we aren't required to get a room number or anything, so I couldn't swear to it."

I thanked her and left. When I glanced back, she was standing near the sweater rack again, posed and unmoving. Maybe I just imagined a hint of loneliness in her posture.

I figured I'd get more information from the hotel operator by using an inside phone line than I would by walking up to a desk clerk. Besides that, I could feel grains of sand working their way into unmentionable places inside my suit. I needed to get out of it.

The door to my room had no sooner clicked shut behind me than I began to strip out of the cover-up and bikini. Brushing grains of sand away from the tender spot, I picked up the phone.

"What room is Gilbert Page in, please?" I asked the operator when she answered after three rings.

"Ten-fifty-nine — I'll ring," her singsong voice was cut off by the immediate connection.

I let it ring twice, then hung up. After all, *I* knew Gilbert Page wasn't in. Apparently, the hotel didn't know it yet, though.

I wondered about Susan, the companion. Was she traveling with him, or had she made his acquaintance here? I pondered the possibilities as I stepped into the shower.

Ten minutes later, wrapped in a thick hotel terry robe, with one of their equally thick towels around my dripping hair, I picked up the phone book. It was only six. I thought if I could reach Drake Langston I might invite him for a drink as an excuse for giving him the information I had learned so far.

He was listed in the book, but there was no answer when I tried the number. He had said he might be tied up with the police until late.

Deciding to do a little more snooping on my own, I put on a floral print cotton dress and my dressy sandals. I locked my room, leaving one lamp on, and took the elevator to the tenth floor.

As luck would have it, there were two maid's carts in the hall. I love staying at a hotel classy enough to give turn-down service. If most of the guests hadn't gone out for dinner yet, they soon would. I spotted the door to room ten-fifty-nine, and wondered whether Page's companion, Susan, was in there.

I had backtracked five or six rooms down the hall, when a maid stepped out directly across from me, bumping my shoulder. I don't know which of us was more startled. She lowered her eyes, and began making apologetic noises. I assured her I was fine.

She was a tiny older woman, mid-fifties at least, with dark brown skin deeply creased with wrinkles. Her short black hair sat like a puffy shower cap on top of her head. The name badge pinned to her pink uniform told me she was Geraldine.

"Have you done ten-fifty-nine yet?" I asked.

"Mista Page?" Her English might be heavily accented, but there was no mistaking the look that crossed her face.

I dropped my voice, implying confidentiality. "Is he in the room now?"

She shook her head, no, but seemed reluctant to say more. I scrounged in my purse, and came up with a ten dollar bill. It worked like the key to a floodgate.

"I don't clean Mister Page room 'less he leave the sign out."

I had to almost read her lips to follow the quick pidgin.

"The other day? I tap on the door an' use my key to go in?" She drew herself up to her full four foot ten, hands planted firmly on her hips. "Mister Page, he *scream* at me. Yell never come in that room unless he say."

She wagged her index finger in my face. "So, I don't. He no get clean towels at night, and no orchid for the lady."

"What about the lady?" I asked.

She clamped her wrinkled lips together in a straight line, her head nodding knowingly. "Miss Turner. Registered in ten-fifty-seven. But those two rooms connect. Like Mister Page and Miss Turner connect. You know what I mean?" She held two fingers up, pressed together tightly.

I gave her a knowing look. I pretty well had the picture.

"Last night, whee, they have a big fight."

"Oh?"

"That man gotta temper, ya know? He scream at her, then slam the door when he leave."

"When was this?"

"Last night. Oh, 'bout seven-thirty, eight. Me and Hazel up here makin' our rounds like now. Mos' guests out for dinner. I was in ten-fifty-four. Door open, but he no see me."

"Any other visitors last night?"

"Not that I seen."

"Well, thank you, Geraldine. You've been most helpful."

I took the elevator down to ground level, and located a place to have dinner. The most casual of the hotel's many restaurants was open-air, facing the pool. Apparently, they catered mostly to the lunch crowd.

Aside from a couple of families with children and a few singles like myself, the place was quiet. I chose a table for one under a little palm frond umbrella. Suddenly, I was ravenous. I placed my order, then sat back to watch the people walk by.

I thought about Gilbert Page, a man with a temper, apparently generous with money, reminiscent of a slick TV personality.

The waiter brought my salad. He was a good-looking blond guy, no more than twenty-two or -three, probably working this and two other jobs to afford the lifestyle in paradise. I watched people while I finished my salad, an interesting mixture of greens, topped with a tangy sweet-and-sour mango dressing.

A couple about my age circled the pool, hand in hand. They looked like honeymooners. I let myself wonder what it would be like to have someone I planned to spend my whole life with. I'd made it through my first thirty years without a partner. Adding someone now might feel really strange.

The lobster arrived just then, and it seemed like a better

thing to devote my time to than worrying over biological clocks and retirement plans.

Anyway, thoughts about the dead Gilbert Page wouldn't seem to leave me alone. After dinner I would try once again to reach Drake Langston.

It was a little before nine when I got back to the room.

"Hi, Charlie. I got in just a bit ago," he replied to my greeting. He didn't seem surprised to hear from me.

"Have you had dinner yet?" I asked.

"Yeah, I grabbed a burger, and ate it on the way home. In fact, I just stepped out of the shower."

I worked to suppress the image that flashed before me. "How about coffee? I've learned a few things about our dead man."

"Give me thirty minutes to throw some clothes on and get down there. I'll meet you at the top of the escalator."

Drake looked just as good in an aloha shirt of muted colors and white slacks as he had wearing work clothes earlier in the day. I watched him enter the lobby; he smiled quickly at an elderly couple and flashed a "hang loose" sign at the bellman before he saw me standing near the escalator.

Again, that dazzling smile as his eyes coursed appreciatively over my attire. He placed a gentle hand on my elbow as we walked back through the lobby. His white Datsun mini-pickup was parked out front.

"Did you have a particular place in mind?" he asked.

"I'm not familiar with anything here, so you lead the way."

We drove through a maze of winding narrow roads, without leaving the hotel grounds, stopping in front of a place called the Inn on the Cliffs.

Inn on the Cliffs was more like the sitting room in some incredibly wealthy person's mansion than a restaurant. Comfortable groupings of furniture clustered around a large fireplace. Gas logs glowed, taking the nip out of the ocean breeze that came through double doors leading to a small lanai. We settled into wing chairs upholstered in a pattern of little flowers.

A three piece group played soft love songs from the forties and fifties.

A blond waitress in a short ruffled skirt brought a dessert tray by, and I couldn't resist the treacherous-looking chocolate torte. Drake was a bit more restrained with his choice of fruit strudel.

Between bites of heavenly chocolate, I related to him what I'd learned that afternoon.

"I'm impressed," he said, pouring a whirl of cream from a silver pitcher onto the surface of his coffee. "I don't think the police even have the identity of the man yet.

"It was fairly clear to me that the guy died from a blow to the head, whether inflicted by a person, or by falling out there on the Na Pali, I couldn't say for sure. I didn't see any footprints around the guy, no blood on the ground or the rocks but it just wasn't a normal place for someone to be walking."

"So maybe he was hit on the head somewhere else, and dumped there?" I mumbled the words through a mouthful of thick chocolate.

He shrugged. "We took the body to Kauai General Hospital, and I'm pretty sure Akito is ordering an autopsy.

"Jack Akito is the officer assigned to the case. I think you should go talk to him in the morning, Charlie. They need all the help they can get around here."

He accented the words by jabbing his fork into the air.

I let the comment go, busying myself with a sip of coffee. There's no more unwelcome feeling than you get when involving yourself in a police case where you know more about it than they do.

I haven't seen a cop yet who warms up to such a situation.

We sat awhile longer, enjoying the music and the warmth

from the fireplace. I noticed that Drake seemed to be a little tired around the edges, so I suggested we leave.

"Guess I better," he agreed. "I'm flying again tomorrow."

There was a three-quarter moon out as we strolled across the parking lot toward his truck. The smell of plumeria filled the air. I found it incredibly romantic. It took a tangible force of will not to reach out and touch him.

I wondered whether he noticed.

We drove back to the hotel's main entrance, each intent on our own thoughts. Our silence was comfortable as we strolled through the upper lobby and rode the escalator down. He walked me across the thick Oriental rug in the lower lobby, past the richly polished teak front desk, over to the elevators. He offered to see me up to my room, but I knew he was also anxious to get some sleep, so I declined.

"After tomorrow, I have four days off," he said. "Can I call you?"

I nodded. He squeezed my hand, and walked back to the escalator. I watched the moving stairs carry him upward before I turned toward the elevators.

In my room, I found my bed turned down and an orchid on my pillow.

4

Jack Akito reacted to my news just about the way I expected he would.

He was a middle-aged man who obviously had very Oriental ideas about a woman's place, which wasn't in *his* police station.

I had squeezed the rental car into the last available space in the parking lot beside the cinderblock building. The station was one story, painted blotchy off-yellow, about the color of dried urine. Orange scallops decorated the base of the building, where the sprinklers had splattered rusty red earth up on the walls. Some scrawny ti plants attempted to survive the wind that whipped them against the cinderblock.

A couple of women sat on the concrete steps, possibly waiting for visiting hours to begin. A uniformed officer stood outside the front door. He lit up a cigarette just as I passed him. I almost held my breath, but he turned away from me to exhale.

It had taken fifteen minutes to get escorted back to Akito's desk. Now I felt like I was stuck in the Oriental version of a Mexican standoff.

"I am sorry, madam, but a murder investigation here on Kauai is no concern of yours," Akito told me.

He remained as polite, as smooth-faced, and as unwavering as a block wall. His dark uniform looked stifling to me in the heavy humid air, but he seemed unaffected. Every crease held its shape, and his tie was knotted precisely. His badge hung perfectly straight. His narrow eyes never wavered.

The Caucasian officer at the adjoining desk was obviously an old timer in the department. I noticed him watching our exchange. Although his stripes indicated his rank was lower than Akito's, he butted right in.

"Listen sweetie," he interjected, "we know our jobs here, and when we want advice from an outsider, we'll ask for it."

His tactfulness certainly left something to be desired. I couldn't believe the nerve of the guy. Actually, I couldn't believe Akito let the remarks pass.

I gritted my teeth. I have a real problem with being called sweetie, honey, baby, or dearie. Especially when it comes from a man who's too old to be my boyfriend and too young to be my father. If my eyes could emit laser beams, his throat would have been in mortal danger.

I forced the corners of my mouth upward, but my teeth refused to unclench.

Akito sat, implacable.

"Fine," I said, working to keep my voice a monotone. "I came here because Drake Langston thinks I have information you could use."

Officer Rudeness piped in again. "Oh, he does, huh? What could a helicopter pilot and a little haole tourist know about this?"

"We know more about it than you do at this point."

I fought to keep my voice level. I could feel my neck getting hot, my self control slipping.

"If you want my help, I'm willing to give it." I stared at the rude one. "If not, then personally, I don't give a damn what you do."

I turned to leave and saw Akito swallw a couple of times, quickly. His eyes widened slightly as he took a deep breath.

"Wait." I could tell by the tone that it was killing his manly pride to utter the word.

I turned slowly, and zoomed him with the laser beam eyes again.

"Miss . . . Parker," he began, emerging from behind his desk. "Your friend is right. We welcome information which might help us solve a crime."

Akito looked rather pitiful. He was struggling not to grovel.

The other officer was shifting from one foot to the other. Akito's turn-around let him know that his own remarks would come back to haunt him later. I kept my distance. It took a real force of will to unclench my teeth.

"The victim's name is Gilbert Page. He's registered at the Westin." I turned toward the door again. "And you can damn well find out the rest on your own."

My heart pounded as I got back to my car, and my hand had a hard time fitting the key into the ignition. The tires chirped as I jammed the car into reverse.

By the time I had swung out of my parking space, and into the traffic on Umi Street, I realized that I was in no condition to drive. I found a shady spot in the parking lot of the public library a block away and pulled in.

I turned off the ignition with shaky fingers, took a deep breath, and rested my forehead on the steering wheel.

Smart, Charlie. Real smart.

I hate scenes. Flashes of my parents screaming at each other bounced back at me.

Why had I taken the bait? Why hadn't I let him save face, condescend a bit, then let me tell my story?

Because I'm quick to get defensive, I guess. Growing up with two older brothers constantly picking on me, it just seems to come naturally.

I pushed the button to lower the convertible top, and pulled my hair up to let the breeze cool the back of my neck. Why had I shot back that last remark?

It's not smart to antagonize a cop. Now that I'd pissed him off, he'd probably drag me in for questioning.

Well — day two of my vacation.

I closed my eyes for a couple of minutes, forcing my mind to go blank. I was breathing better now, and decided I couldn't let the whole day fall apart.

It wasn't yet noon. I'd go back to the hotel, grab my beach stuff, and try to make up for lost time. That way, if the golden dragon did decide to haul me in, at least I would have managed one day of sunshine on the trip.

The message light on my phone was blinking when I got in. Drake Langston, wondering if I was free for dinner.

I left a message with Melanie at Paradise's office that yes, I was. Things were starting to look up.

I flipped through the hangers in the closet. Yes, the emerald green silk would do for tonight, a blend of classy and naughty. The color always looked good with my dark auburn hair, and it brought out the green in my eyes.

I ran my fingers through my hair. Maybe I should try to do something with it, set it or something. But, with the humidity here, it would just be straight again in no time. I decided not to bother. Those details out of the way, I put on my bikini and a big shirt, and gathered sunscreen, glasses, and my book.

Between the hoard of teenagers whooping it up at the volleyball net, and the family with three gooey-faced shriekers, the beach lost some of its appeal. Besides, I wasn't sure I relished the idea of more sand in the suit. Lounge chairs and cold drinks sounded better, so I opted for the pool instead.

There were probably two hundred people present, whose lounge chairs circled the freeform pool like cars at the drive-in theater. Even so, there were whole sections unoccupied. I prefer my Tom Clancy undisturbed, so I snagged a waiter, ordered a mai-tai, and pointed out a nearly empty section.

The pool was a winding thing which circled a little island containing more lounge chairs and a few palm trees. I watched a hunky guy with a great set of lungs swim the whole thing under water. He only had to come up for air three times.

The hotel's buildings surrounded the pool area on three sides, the other side being the opening to the beach. The whole courtyard was ringed by a colonnade with fat white pillars holding up its roof. Under this roof, the non sun-lovers could sink back into cushy upholstered couches and chairs, and get the feeling they were at the pool without taking any chances.

Periodically, the white pillars veered from their orderly circle to bulge out and form the roof over a bubbling hot tub. I counted five such cauldrons.

All this nudged nicely into an area slightly smaller than three football fields. I realized I better keep close count of the mai tais or I wouldn't have the stamina for the hike back to the elevators.

Three chapters into Clancy, I flipped from my back onto my tummy, and three chapters later figured I'd better exit. It would not do to let a massive sunburn ruin the evening. I switched to a chair in the shade, and did a slow cool down before going inside.

Back in my room, I indulged in a soothing shower and a short nap before slipping on the green dress. By six o'clock I was ready to meet Drake in the lobby.

He was handsome as ever in a different print shirt and white slacks, which I gathered was standard attire here, anytime day or night.

After ascertaining that I was game for almost any kind of food, he took me to the Japanese Tea House. Except for the bar just inside the front door, it was built like a real Japanese house, or as close to one as I'd ever seen.

A series of small rooms, open on one side, faced into a small courtyard garden, where small paths led over miniature bridges to scaled-down groupings of plants. The other three walls of each room were those kind that look like lightweight wooden frames with paper stretched over them. Surprisingly, it felt very private.

The table was low with cushions on the floor around it. My old stretched knee ligament groaned at the sight. But the seating was a trick. There was a pit under the table which allowed us to sit at floor level with our legs under the table, as if we were in chairs. My opinion of Officer Akito's forebears rose several points.

We shared small talk over a plate of sushi appetizers. Drake was in a good mood, I gathered, because he now had four days off. I related the gist of my meeting with the police, leaving out a few of the choicer words.

"Akito's got it in for the helicopter operators, anyway," he told me. "He's probably just pissed that we're the ones who found the body."

"But, why? You helped make his job a little easier, is all."

"Loss of face. It's important here."

I pondered that.

"Besides," he continued, "Akito and Mack had a run-in a few years ago. I don't even remember what it was about now. Mack and I were friends, but it was before I came to work for him. Whatever it was though, the wound is still festering. Believe me, there is no love lost between those two."

"Well, I can see Mack's side of it. Akito is not exactly a warm and friendly kind of guy. I'd just as soon not have my encounter at the police station be my strongest memory of my week on Kauai."

His eyes held mine with a tangible firmness. The candlelight softened his features and illuminated his smile. I swallowed hard. Suddenly, a week wasn't long enough, even if we could have magically created seventy-two hour days.

"Tell me about Charlie Parker," he said, easing us away from a very intense moment.

"Charlotte Louise Parker was born in Albuquerque, New Mexico, thirty years ago. I was the youngest of three, and the only girl. I suppose I could have grown up fluffy and spoiled, but with two brothers as my influence, it didn't work out that way. I was a tough little tomboy."

I caught him glancing at the low-cut neckline on my dress. He smiled. I cleared my throat.

"Seems like you outgrew the tomboy stage pretty well," he commented.

I could feel a red flush creep up my face. I pulled my square wooden chopsticks from the wrapper, and rubbed them together between my palms.

"My brothers are okay now, you understand. They were just normal boys. Paul is married. Lives in Phoenix. Ron is my partner in the agency. They're both good guys. I think they took out all their childhood aggressions on me."

He chuckled. "I know. I guess I was the same way with my sister. What about your parents?"

"My father was a physicist at Sandia Labs. My mother was a country-clubber whose family never let her forget that she had married way beneath them. To them, even a scientist with a PhD was still a working slob. Mother and Dad were killed in a plane crash."

He started to say something sympathetic, but I didn't give him the chance.

"I was sixteen, and I suppose I should have been traumatized by it but truthfully, the silence was kind of nice. They left me the house, and enough money to get by on."

I didn't think it was the time to tell him that "enough" meant a good-sized portfolio of blue chip stocks. Guys' personalities tend to undergo radical changes when they find out you have a little nest egg. I helped myself to two more tempura shrimp and another spoonful of some wonderfully gingery vegetable dish.

"So now you investigate things for supplemental income, or just for the sheer fun of it?"

"Some of each, I guess." I related the story of how I'd saved Mrs. Higgins from her insurance agent. "She's like a grandmother to me. Watches out for me like I was her own, and she takes care of Rusty for me when I travel."

"Rusty? Your child?"

"My dog."

He smiled at that.

I told him a little about Rusty, and what a softie he really is. The garden outside our little cubicle was quiet, softly lit along its pathways. Miniature plants circled a small pond whose waterfall flowed soothingly. Drake's eyes met mine and I had a strong sense that the attraction between us was mutual.

"I've only come close to matrimony once." I confessed. "I was engaged to my college sweetheart, Brad North. Two weeks before the wedding, he eloped with my best friend, Stacy.

"They live in a great big house in the most exclusive part of town. Brad's a lawyer now. She drives a Mercedes, wears hunks of diamonds on both hands, belongs to the country club, and looks absolutely terrified whenever dear old Brad walks into the room. He's put on thirty pounds since I knew him; she has chronic dark circles under her eyes, and I hear she practically lives on Valium. I shudder to think how close I came to having all that."

He took my hand across the table. "I'm glad Brad and Stacy eloped, too."

Dessert consisted of little squares of something white and sticky and sweet enough to please even me.

Drake drove back to the hotel by way of the small boat harbor. A sultry tropic breeze caressed my neck while we stood for a few moments on the pier. Lights across the harbor shot wavy ribbons of silver and gold out over the dark water.

Small sailboats rocked gently in their slips, mooring lines creaking rhythmically. The barges and cargo vessels were dark hulks, lacking activity, lit only by sodium vapor lights lining the dock's walkways.

In general, the area was quiet this time of night, although we caught fragments of rock music from a club somewhere in the distance. He put his arm around my shoulders and I leaned into the comfort of it.

This time, he rode the elevator with me to the seventh floor. I handed him my door key, and he graciously unlocked it. His kiss was warm, making my insides feel the way hot fudge looks when it slides off the ice cream and forms a puddle in the dish. He broke away before I was quite ready.

"I'll call you tomorrow. Maybe we can take a ride up into the mountains?"

I ran my fingers down the right side of his face, and nodded. I stepped into my room and the door clicked firmly between us. This was best. I'd already opened up to him more than I usually do. Must be the tropical air.

I washed my face, brushed my teeth, and fell into a pleasant saki-laden sleep, the faint scent of Drake's after-shave clinging to my hair.

The ringing of the telephone was harsh and sudden, and I bounded up off the pillow before I had regained consciousness. My heart pounded so hard I could feel it in my limbs, and it took me several seconds to figure out where I was. The flashing red message light led me to the offensive instrument.

"Hello?" My throat was thick with sleep, and only the last part of the word came out.

"Charlie, it's Drake."

"Drake, what is it?" My fingers reached for the lamp, almost knocking its oversized shade off. The sudden light made my eyes slam back shut. My fingers groped around on the nightstand for my travel alarm. Three o'clock. Ugh.

" . . . been arrested on suspicion of murder."

I dragged myself back to the voice inside the receiver. "Wait, Drake, what?"

"Mack! Mack has been arrested for the murder."

5

"When did this happen?" My brain cells were finally beginning minimal function.

"Around midnight, I guess."

At midnight, he had been kissing me at my door.

"Mack said the police came to his house late, and took him downtown. They just now let him use the phone. Like he was a menace to society, or something. Charlie, this is ridiculous. I've got to help him."

I struggled to think. There wasn't much we could do in the middle of the night, and I told him so. I suggested that he meet me here at the hotel at six, and we'd go to the station together. Surely, someone would be there so we could post bond by seven or so. I could tell he was anxious to do something right away, but he grudgingly agreed.

I set the travel alarm for five-thirty, and fell back on my pillow, wondering how I manage to get so entangled in other people's problems. I only wanted a vacation . . .

The alarm rang so quickly, I thought I had mistakenly set the time wrong. But, no. It really was five-thirty. I toyed with the idea of pretending I hadn't heard it, but gave it up.

Whether or not I got involved in Mack Garvey's problems, I did want to see Drake again. As irritating as it was to think of Akito and Mack and their little squabble, I could appreciate Drake's loyalty to his friend.

He was waiting for me in the lobby, and I suggested that we find some coffee before we tackled the forces in blue. I reasonably pointed out that it was unlikely that we'd get much action at the station before seven, and I don't function at all well in the mornings without fuel. Besides, having breakfast would give him a chance to fill me in on whatever I'd better know before going up against Akito again.

Outside, the sky was pearl gray, the sun not fully up yet. Banks of low dark clouds squatted on the horizon. It was impossible to tell whether they would later move toward us, or away. Rust colored mud puddles lined the uncurbed streets, the remains of showers that had moved through sometime during the night. The streets were quiet, traffic at a minimum in the pre-dawn. The street lights began to shut off, one by one, as we left the main drag and wound our way among the side streets.

A round woman in a purple flowered mumu stood in her front yard and called to a little dog who was paying not the slightest attention as he trotted away from her.

At the next house, a sleepy-looking man with tousled hair padded out to the sidewalk in his rubber flip-flops. He gazed around, perhaps searching for his morning paper. We passed before he found it.

Drake took me to a tan cinderblock structure called the Tip Top Bakery and Cafe. Paint flaked from the 50s style building, leaving chips on the sidewalk and surrounding shrubbery like dirty snow. Drake turned into the parking lot slowly, guiding the truck between potholes. He assured me that inside it was much less scary than it looked. I had to take his word for it — nothing else was open.

There were only three cars in the lot at this hour. Drake pulled his mini-pickup in beside them. They were obviously all locals, not a red tourist convertible in sight.

There was a hulking old Plymouth Barracuda just outside my door. Its door frame was intact, but not much else was. Ragged bands of rust outlined the doors and the car's top. In its advanced stage of leprosy, parts could begin falling off at any time. I opened my door carefully to avoid touching it. It was probably contagious, and I didn't want to take chances with Drake's truck.

Inside, the cafe was one large room, divided into a small section and a large one. The small side held a couple of bakery cases and a shelf unit, empty now except for one loaf of bread apparently left from yesterday. Heavenly smells from the kitchen indicated that the shelves would soon be refilled.

A long counter with a dozen short stools in front of it ran the length of the back wall. Two of the stools were occupied by men in work clothes. Each man had a cup of coffee, a donut, and an open newspaper in front of him.

The remaining large section of the room was filled with formica tables in assorted sizes. Either they catered to big families, or the banquet business was pretty hot. Several of the tables were set to accommodate ten or twelve people.

We took a booth near the windows, three booths away from the only other patrons in the place. The vinyl seat was cracked in a pattern like a broken windshield. The backs of my legs were thankful I hadn't worn shorts. Drake recommended the

51

macadamia nut pancakes and coffee and that sounded good to me.

"Okay," I began once the waitress had left, "what evidence do they have against Mack?"

He sighed: "Because there were no footprints around the body, and it was nowhere near the hiking trail, they conclude that the man was dropped from a helicopter."

"That's not evidence! That's what my eighth grade math teacher used to call a WEG, a Wild-Eyed Guess. No way they can hold him on that."

"There's more. They found blood in the ship."

"Mack's helicopter? Have they matched the type to the victim? Did Mack have any explanation for it?"

"I don't know," he said miserably. "We only got to speak for a minute last night. He couldn't really tell me anything."

I reached out to touch the back of his hand. Clearly, he was upset about the mess Mack was in, and I wasn't helping much. All I could do was try to reassure him that it would all work out.

"Tell me more about Mack."

"He's been in his own business here about five years. I've worked for him three. I think he's a pretty straightforward guy. Competition here is fierce, and Mack is a scrapper. But I know he's honest, and he works hard for what he's got. He learned to fly in Vietnam, and has been at it ever since. He's flown all over the world."

"What about his personal life?"

"Single, no kids. I think there was a brief marriage years ago, but he never talks about it. A helicopter pilot's nomad life doesn't lend itself to lasting relationships."

Drake's eyes focused briefly on a spot out in the middle of the room, then he busied himself putting sugar in his coffee. He didn't elaborate and I didn't ask.

"Mack's got his problems, but basically he's a good guy to work for. He gave me a job during an especially bad time in my life, and he's always been fair with me."

The pancakes arrived then, and we devoted our attention to them. They were heavenly — slightly crisp on the surface, with generous bits of macadamia nuts inside. I smothered mine with pink guava jam.

"How did you get into flying helicopters?" I asked Drake. Our initial hunger had been satisfied and we'd both paused between bites.

"Vietnam, like most everyone," he replied. "After that, I put in quite a few years in South America, the Gulf of Mexico, the Rockies."

"Sounds dangerous."

"I've lost a lot of friends over the years." He chewed slowly, remembering long-gone faces.

"Have you had a lot of close calls yourself?" I pictured scenes of violent fiery crashes like in the movies.

He shrugged. "I guess I'm more cautious than most. I check every aircraft I get into; I preflight them as though each flight were the first. I've caught a lot of potential mechanical failures that way. But it's hard to catch them all. I've had six engine failures over the years."

My hand stopped midway to my coffee cup.

"Yes, I'm still here to tell about it," he chuckled. He patted my hand. "A helicopter's a bit different than an airplane. We execute a procedure called autorotation. As long as we have a reasonably flat open space it's not difficult to make a safe landing. And you can bet I practice it with every new aircraft I get into."

He spoke offhandedly enough that I felt at ease. Obviously, he knew what he was doing. The conversation turned back to Mack and his problems while we finished the last of our coffee.

The sun was fully up when we emerged from the Tip Top. Traffic rushed by, cars in a big hurry to carry their owners to work. Drake guided his truck down Akahi street, made two or three short turns and pulled in at the police station. The yellowed cinderblock structure looked just the same as the last time I'd visited — was it really less than twenty-four hours ago? — but there were very few cars in the lot and no women waiting on the front steps.

An hour later, we had Mack out on bond and were seated in his office. Although I had met him only briefly two days before, he looked ten years older than I remembered. The fluorescent office lighting cast a harsh glare on his face, accentuating an underlying grayness in his skin. The furrows between his brows had grown deeper and the outer corners of the brown eyes drooped downward in resignation.

The man was worried.

He was clearly in no shape to fly tours, so Drake offered to take the first one of the day. Melanie would rearrange the rest of the day's schedule.

Drake left to preflight the aircraft, and I decided I better get to know everything I could about Mack Garvey. Naturally, my first question was whether he even wanted my help. I wanted to think that I could easily walk out, and spend the rest of my week guilt-free on the beach. Sometimes I curse this soft spot I seem to have for a guy who's getting an unfair shake.

"Drake seems to have a lot of faith in you," he told me wearily. "And it's a safe bet that Akito won't be looking to clear me. He's already puffed up thinking he's solved the case."

"But, Mack, without evidence they won't get a conviction. A decent lawyer would have you off in no time."

"Yeah. That sounds good in theory, but there are a few things you don't understand about life in the islands. There's a good-old-boy system here that rivals anything I've ever seen.

If your last name isn't Fujimoto or Nakamura or . . . well, you get the idea, then you ain't in.

"A white boy like me, a haole, is a foreigner. Doesn't matter that I've been here ten years, I'm still the newcomer. Finding an attorney that would really go to bat for me will be tough. Drake told me a little about your background. I'd really appreciate anything you could do for me. I'll be glad to pay you, reimburse your expenses, whatever."

"I'm doing this as a favor to Drake," I told him, trying to ignore his obvious prejudices. "Although you might rather hire yourself a local investigator, someone who knows the situation here better than I do."

He sighed deeply. "That's about the same as hiring a local attorney. There's only one PI firm here on the island, and the guy is in really tight with Akito. No way he'd save my skin.

"Besides that, Charlie, no matter what the verdict, just going to trial will cost me my business. Word gets around. I'll lose all the contacts I've carefully built, those who send customers my way. I can't afford not to be out there flying."

His voice cracked, and I stared down at my fingers. The poor guy really was desperate.

"Okay, then, let's get down to business. Tell me everything the police have. Then tell me everything you know that the police don't know yet." I had the distinct feeling there was more to this story than Drake comprehended.

Mack buzzed Melanie on the intercom, and asked her to bring coffee. He closed his door softly behind her after she delivered the two cups. I stirred two lumps of sugar into mine, giving him a few moments to put his thoughts together.

"The police believe the body was dropped from a helicopter, because of the remote location," he began. "It was too far inland to have washed up from the sea. The Kalalau hiking trail does go up that valley, but the body was way off the trail, several hundred yards, in fact. They say the guy died as a result of a blow to the back of the head. Seems to me, if he had wandered off the trail, and fallen off one of those rugged peaks, there would have been bruises and scrapes all over the body. But they said there was only the one injury.

"The terrain was too rugged for a landing, but they figure a helicopter could fly in there and hover a few feet off the ground, and drop a body out." He paused, staring at the wall.

"I guess the other incriminating thing they have that ties me in is the blood they found in my aircraft."

"What can you tell me about that?"

"Same thing I told them. On my last flight Friday, the day before the body was found, a little girl sitting in the back seat had a gusher of a nosebleed. Her mother managed to get it stopped, so it didn't become a medical emergency, but she did leave a pretty good sized spot on my carpet. It was the end of the day, and my mechanic wasn't around, so I cleaned it up the best I could. I figured I'd get him out there in the morning with some of that super cleaner he has, to work on it some more. By the next morning, it had slipped my mind."

"Any chance of finding the girl and her mother to verify that?"

"I doubt it." His shoulders sagged. "I had Melanie look back over Friday's manifest. The woman's name was Linda Smith, from Los Angeles. They were a walk-in so we didn't get their hotel, and they paid cash. By now, there's a good chance they've left the island."

"Well, there are always DNA tests, Mack. It can be proven that it wasn't Page's blood," I pointed out.

"Yeah, but I can't afford to let it go that far. Like I said, even the hint of involvement in this could put me out of business."

I jotted some notes in a little spiral I always carry with me, and tried to imagine a possible sequence of events that would tie in with what Mack was telling me.

"Mack, wouldn't it be physically impossible for one man to fly a helicopter, and push a body out the door? I mean, you have to keep your hands and feet on the controls at all times, don't you?"

"Exactly. That's what I tried to tell Akito." He stood up abruptly, and paced to the far side of the room. "That's the frustrating thing. They just wouldn't listen to me."

"So, how do they think you might have accomplished the deed?"

"With the help of my mechanic, Joe Esposito. We had scheduled maintenance at the hangar that evening. Joe was supposed to change a tail rotor blade that had developed some hairline cracks in the laminate, and then I was to come out and start the aircraft, so we could track the blades."

"So you were both at the hangar that night?"

"Well, that's the thing. I never did see Joe. I finished my last flight, and left the ship parked at the hangar. I grabbed a box of chicken at Kentucky Fried, and came to the office to do some FAA paperwork. Normally, Joe would do the work, then call me either here or at home to let me know when he was ready for me."

"But he didn't call?"

"Drake called about ten o'clock. Teased me about burning the midnight oil, and told me I was wearing myself too thin. He suggested that I go on home. He could come out early the next morning and do the tracking before the first flight. Truth is, I *was* beat. I'd just done three days in a row, seven flights a day. It didn't take much to convince me. I tried to phone Joe at the hangar, and let him know the plan. When there was no answer, I went on home."

"Have the police talked to Joe?"

"I don't know."

"Okay, Mack, now I need to know the rest. You knew Gilbert Page, didn't you?"

He stared out the window, toward the airport. I could hear rotor blades in the distance. He was struggling to decide how much he should tell.

"Mack," I said, trying to keep my voice gentle, "you might as well tell me all of it. You can bet the police will find out, anyway. I can't help you if you withhold information."

He came back to his chair, and flopped heavily into it. He ran his fingers through his hair, then leaned his chin against his entwined fingers. His eyes closed for a moment, while he took a deep breath.

"Yes, I knew Gilbert Page." His voice had a ragged weariness to it.

I felt sorry for him.

"I met him about three years ago at a helicopter convention in Las Vegas. He had money and was looking to invest in some type of helicopter operation. My old aircraft was really tired. It was to a point where I'd either have to put about two hundred grand into a major overhaul on it, or replace it. Going to the convention is like visiting a new car dealer's showroom, while your old clunker sits out in the parking lot. I wanted one of those new ships with all the bells and whistles. I must have been practically drooling.

"Gil had real business savvy, and we really hit it off. He offered to put up five hundred thousand, and I'd use my two-fifty."

I did a mental *whoa*. Seven hundred fifty grand for one of those little whirlybirds? I know I'd counted around twenty of them out at the heliport. Fifteen million or so, just sitting out there on the ground.

"Gil said he didn't want to get involved with the daily operations of the business. He had plenty else going on in California where he came from. We would treat the money strictly as an equipment loan. That was fine with me. I didn't want a partner trying to butt in and tell me how to run my business. I can see now that I had stars in my eyes when I signed the contract. I didn't realize that the interest rate he wanted was almost twice what the regular aircraft financing companies were charging at the time. And I didn't pay much attention to the clause that allowed him to call in the loan, in full, at any time."

"So Gil came here, pressuring you for the balance, and you didn't have it."

He nodded, staring at a distant point on the carpet.

"And, I don't suppose you could have borrowed it from somewhere else? Or satisfied him with part of it?"

He pulled himself up, waving one hand vaguely. "Well, of course I have contacts."

He seemed about to go on in that vein, but suddenly slumped again. "Gil just never gave me a chance to work anything out. He wanted all the money, and he wanted it right then."

I could see that he was emotionally drained. I closed my notebook, and sat with him in silence for a few minutes. It's a terrible thing to watch a man's dream fade away.

Finally, he spoke: "Charlie, I began to see Gilbert Page, not as the savior of my business dreams, but as a slick con man, with degrading tactics and a terrible temper. I grew to hate him, but I didn't kill him — I swear I didn't. I need your help."

It wasn't going to be easy. Money is a powerful motivator, and Mack had about five hundred thousand reasons to want Gil off his back. That fact, coupled with an old-time grudge with the police, didn't make Mack's situation look any too hopeful.

I felt sorry for him, but then, in this business, it's seldom that I don't feel bad for the clients and the messes they get themselves into. I left Mack sitting at his desk, his fingers rubbing at his weary eyes.

Mack's shuttle driver gave me a lift back to the hotel, where I retrieved my rental from the parking lot. Mack hadn't given me a lot to go on, so I thought I'd see if I could find out what the police knew. It might give me an edge.

I also wanted to search out anyone I could find locally who had known Gil Page.

Kauai General Hospital was only three or four blocks from Paradise's office, a modern four-story structure of gray concrete with deep blue stucco acents. The visitor's lot was about half full. It was a little before ten o'clock.

Three hours or so into the morning shift, those with seniority might be taking a few minutes extra on their coffee breaks, leaving junior staffers, or perhaps nobody, in charge.

I felt like a kid on her first day in a new school. I knew the general routine, but it varies from one town to the next. I was nervous that a procedural faux pas would send me to Principal Akito's office.

I took a chance that the morgue would be in the basement. Riding the elevator down, I formulated a plan.

Luckily, I had dressed in a linen suit this morning. I snagged an empty clipboard from an unattended counter top, and stopping at a ladies room on the way, I rooted around in my bag for a few items of costume. I pulled my shoulder length straight hair into a ponytail at the nape of my neck, and held it in place with a fabric covered stretchy band. Non-prescription horn rimmed glasses helped convey an air of authority, I hoped. I stuck a few sheets of paper into the clipboard, my car rental receipt, and the Westin's List of Guest Services, among them.

Well, I would just hold it close to my chest.

Coming off the elevator, I had noticed a discreet sign indicating that the morgue was down the hall to my right. I emerged from the ladies room, and headed that direction, looking much more confident than I felt.

The basement corridor was quiet and unpopulated. I had not seen anyone since getting off the elevator.

The hallway was tiled in white vinyl, patterned with light blue speckles, and polished to a gloss. Upstairs, the walls had been painted pale blue to coordinate, but down here they were institution tan. There were scuff marks on the walls, just at gurney height — so numerous that I imagined a game of medical bumper cars going on.

All the doors along the corridor were closed, and I could see double swinging doors at the far end, which I presumed to be the morgue. I tried to walk confidently without allowing my shoes to make noise on the shiny tile floor. It isn't easy.

A quick visual survey revealed only one attendant behind the swinging double doors. I hoped to get this over with fast, and be out of there before anyone else showed up. This one was young, twenty-one or -two at most. He was a tall, skinny thing with a sprout of red curls, and freckles so large that they blended together in unusual patches, making me wonder if he was the victim of a dreaded epidermal disease.

I waved my open wallet in his general direction, as I consulted the top sheet on my clipboard.

"I'm investigating the Gilbert Page case. That's P-A-G-E. I need to see the autopsy report, and if you have it, the police report as well." I clamped my lips together tightly, and stood with my arms crossed.

"Yyess, ma'am." He stammered over the words like I was an IRS auditor asking him to show me his dependents. He began clumsily rummaging through a file drawer in the desk.

"Here's the file," he announced, handing it to me.

I flipped it open, and glanced over the pages, tsk-tsked a couple of times, and consulted my clipboard again.

"Already, my secretary has a couple of vital facts wrong. I'll need copies of these for my files. You do have a copier here, don't you?"

"Oh, yes, ma'am."

I shoved the folder toward him. "Fine. The top two pages, please."

He practically went down face first in his attempt to clear his ungainly size twelves from the rolling wheels of his swivel chair. He blushed the color of a ripe watermelon and stumbled into a little room behind him. I glanced at my watch.

Fifteen minutes had passed since I'd entered the building. I wondered if his supervisor would come back any minute now and demand to see my credentials. I willed him to *hurry*.

"Here they are, ma'am," he said, returning from the other room with a neat sheaf of papers.

I tucked the copies safely into my clipboard. "You've been most helpful," I said, gracing him with a smile.

Back in the ladies room, I pulled the papers from the clipboard, and jammed them into my bag. The glasses were beginning to make me feel weird, so I shoved them in there, too.

As nonchalantly as possible, I dropped off the empty clipboard where I had found it, and pressed the elevator button. The girl sitting at the desk didn't even look up.

I waited until I was back in the car to take out the papers and re-read them. It looked like pretty standard stuff. Time of death: between 10 and 12 p.m. Cause of death: blow to the back of the skull with a blunt instrument. Hmm, the proverbial blunt instrument. The police report didn't have any further notation.

So, they didn't know what the weapon was yet either. Victim's blood type was A positive. So common that there was a very good chance it would match the type they found in the helicopter.

I read through the police report twice. I couldn't see anything incriminating enough to warrant throwing Mack in jail at midnight last night. Drake had told me Akito had it in for Mack. I'd say. Back on the mainland, he'd be looking squarely in the face of a false arrest suit.

Something caught my eye that I'd missed the first time through. The body had been identified and claimed by Mrs. Catherine Page. The wife, no doubt. I'd need to find her, and ask some questions before she left the island.

6

I had a hunch about where to reach Mrs. Page, and figured it would be quicker to follow it up by telephone. There was a bank of pay phones right outside the entrance to the hospital.

"Aloha, Westin Kauai." An extremely cordial male voice greeted me. I always picture such voices as belonging to tall, tan guys with muscles like iron. They generally turn out to be short, overweight, and fifty.

"Yes, do you have a Mrs. Catherine Page registered?"

"One moment." The good-looking voice came right back. "Yes, ma'am, she is registered. However, her key is here at the desk, so apparently she is out."

"Thank you, I'll try later."

It figured. Once exposed to the fine life of first class hotels, she was hardly likely to check into a cheap little motel down the street.

I was fairly certain that she would either be at a funeral home arranging for her husband's body to be shipped back to the mainland, or at Akito's office. Since I didn't know what she looked like, I couldn't very well go cruising around town hoping to bump into her somewhere.

It was not even noon yet, but my three a.m. awakening was beginning to tell on me. My eyelids felt droopy, and I had that curious lightheadedness that comes from either lack of sleep or a terrific bender. I sat in the car for a few minutes fighting a strong urge to crawl over into the back seat for a nap.

Maybe I just needed food. It had been almost six hours since breakfast.

I started the car and put the top down. I figured either the wind in my face would refresh me, or the sun on my head would lull me to sleep. I pulled out of the parking lot onto Kuhio Highway.

According to my map, this would eventually lead to Rice Street, and back to the hotel.

Kuhio, I discovered, held Kauai's version of fast food row. I passed up fried chicken and a couple of others before turning in at the golden arches. I took the reports inside with me and pondered over them as I polished off a Big Mac, fries, and a Coke.

I don't know what I expected the reports to yield. They didn't say anything different than they had thirty minutes earlier.

Back at the hotel, I picked up a house phone in the lobby, and used my former ploy to find out Catherine Page's room number. She was on the eighth floor, one above mine.

Apparently, she didn't want to stay in hubby's room which was already paid for. Imagine that.

I knew if I quit moving, I'd be asleep in minutes. Better stick with it. I took the elevator to the eighth floor, watching with longing as my own seventh floor slipped by.

Catherine Page answered the knock on her door so quickly, I almost believed she was expecting someone.

She let me in after giving my business card a cursory tired appraisal. She was about five-four, slim, with medium length hair the drab brown of cardboard. She wore a linen suit in a cream-colored shade with a matching silk blouse, obviously expensive. She had once been an attractive woman, but something was a tad off. The upper eyelids sagged, the mouth was pinched into a thin colorless line. I could see fine blue veins in her throat, making her look fragile.

Her age had been listed on the police report as forty-three, but she sure looked fifty-ish to me. Her nose already showed deep enlarged pores, and her mouth was rimmed by the fine lines of a heavy smoker.

But, there was something else, something in the set of her shoulders. The phrase that leapt to mind was *battle-weary*.

"Would you like a drink?" she offered.

I declined, but told her to go ahead. One drink would put me on my tail in five minutes flat.

She stepped to the mini-bar, and chose a glass. I noticed that she had a full-size bottle of bourbon sitting there. Even the wealthy don't indulge in the outrageous prices of the mini-bar, I guess.

She poured her drink, and lit a fresh cigarette from the butt of the last one, still smoldering in the ashtray.

"I know this is a bad time for you, and I'm sorry to intrude."

I've found when I'm about to intrude on the most personal aspects of someone's life, it's a good idea to at least apologize for doing it.

Her mouth was engaged with the rim of her glass, and she waved one wrist limply toward me, as if to say "no problem."

A small sprinkle of ash drifted down to the carpet. We each took one of the room's upholstered chairs which were about as comfortable as concrete stadium bleachers. I began by explaining that I was gathering evidence in hopes of helping Mack Garvey.

"Were you aware of the purpose of your husband's trip here?"

She huffed a puff of smoke out her nostrils, which I took to be a chuckle. I hadn't meant the question that way, but I realized she knew about Susan Turner.

"I suppose you mean, did I know he was calling on Mack Garvey?" She tapped the cigarette against the edge of the ashtray. "Yes, I did. They had some kind of business deal. I'm not sure what it was. I only met Mack once, on a previous trip to Kauai, although I'm not sure he'd remember me. We stayed here at the Westin, and Gil had invited him to come by for drinks out by the pool. My skin doesn't take the sun well, so I came back inside right after the introductions."

"When was the last time you spoke to your husband?"

"The night he died. Let's see, it was late — probably about eleven o'clock. That would be about eight p.m. here. We talked about our son, Jason."

"Was there anything unusual about the conversation? Did he say anything about Mack?"

The battle weary look came into her eyes, stronger than ever. "No, the conversation was *very* typical."

I studied her face while she drained her drink. She reminded me of a dog I knew once who was kicked around a lot by its owner. It never fought back. It just became resigned to the kicking.

"Tell me about Jason."

Her face softened considerably, and there was almost a hint of a smile at the corners of her mouth. She picked up the ashtray off the table, and made a few seconds of busy work as she elaborately rolled the ash from the end of her cigarette.

"He's twenty. He attended two years at Stanford, and lived on campus there, but now he's back home."

"Which is . . .?"

"Mill Valley. A lovely, quiet spot right outside San Francisco. Anyway, Jason says he's 'bummed out' on school, and wants to take time off. He'd like to try the race car circuit."

"Umm. An expensive hobby, I hear."

"Yes, I suppose so." Her voice was small and drifty again. I got the idea she didn't comprehend that race cars and loaves of bread weren't in the same price range.

"Did Jason overhear that phone conversation between you and Gil?"

"No, he wasn't home. He had stayed over with a friend for a couple of days."

"Male or female?"

"Probably his friend, Mark. They work on their race car together all the time."

Her thoughts turned inward, I could tell, and she smiled indulgently. "Poor little Jennifer. That's the Hightower's daughter, down the road. She's crazy about Jason. What girl wouldn't be? He's a handsome boy. But, he's so wrapped up in that car, he doesn't give her a second glance. She sits around, hoping he'll call her, but he never has the time."

I wondered what any of this had to do with anything, then realized it didn't. Catherine's bourbon was merely rambling.

"I may want to speak with Jason," I interrupted. "How could I get in touch with him?"

She wrote out two numbers for me. One was their home, and the other was for Jason's racing friend, Mark Cramer. She said I would surely find him one place or the other.

There didn't seem to be much more she could tell me and I left a few minutes later.

An eternal optimist, I hoped my luck would hold, and I'd find Susan Turner in. I thought about Catherine Page as I rode the elevator up to the tenth floor.

A simple check of the phone records would confirm whether she had talked to Gil from California that night. She didn't strike me as a wielder of blunt objects, anyway. Still, I couldn't disregard that beaten-pup look. Sometimes the quiet ones will fool you.

And, she certainly had money enough to pay top quality help for any service she needed.

The elevator doors slid open on number ten, and I glanced both ways before stepping out. Susan's room was about four doors down, on the left. As I approached, I realized the young woman walking toward me had just left that room.

"Susan?"

She stopped and appraised me.

She was a big girl, about twenty-four years old, five feet-eight or -nine, I'd guess, and probably a hundred forty pounds, without an ounce of fat on her. She had the solid body of an athlete. Spandex shorts hugged her muscular thighs, and the oversize T-shirt she wore didn't hide the well-developed neck and shoulders. Her long blond hair was pulled back in a neat French braid. Her eyes looked haggard.

"Can we talk a minute?" I showed her my card, and she reopened the door to her room.

She had apparently tried out the concrete bleacher chairs already, because she opted for the bed. Not being familiar enough with her to share the bed, I got stuck with one of the chairs.

"I was just going down to exercise," she said. "Doing aerobics helps me when I feel bad."

Two puddles of moisture pooled in her lower eyelids. Her full lips settled into a little pout, the kind favored by teen models.

"Yes, I imagine it was quite a shock to learn about Gil."

Her lower lip quivered, and she nodded without speaking.

"Look, I won't go through any cute pretenses that you're traveling with Gil as his secretary, or anything. I'm just trying to help a friend. How did you and Gil meet in the first place?"

She went into the bathroom for a Kleenex and came back dabbing at her eyes.

"He used to come into the club where I worked out. In the beginning, he said he was concerned about his cholesterol. He thought aerobics classes would help. We saw each other at class three times a week for over a year."

She wadded the Kleenex into a ball, which she rhythmically squeezed in her palm like a grip strengthener.

"Now I'm opening my own club. Gil was helping with the financing."

I pulled out my little notebook and jotted down the name she gave me. Workout Heaven. Hmm, a complete contradiction in terms, in my mind. She wanted to tell me all about the equipment they had and offered me a free month's membership.

"Sure," I said, "although I don't get to San Francisco too often."

I couldn't admit to her that I don't exercise because I really hate it. My brother, Ron, tells me that attitude will catch up with me one day, probably soon, now that I've hit the big three-oh.

"Tell me more about you and Gil," I prompted.

"We were sleeping together within the first two weeks after we met. His wife is an iceberg. She drinks a lot, which is really terrible for your body, you know. She dotes on that kid, Jason, while she treats Gil like dirt. She nagged at Gil all the time — Jason needs this, Jason needs that. You know what Jason's latest thing is? Race cars. He wanted Daddy to just up and buy him one of those fancy ones, so he could join the circuit. Can you believe it? Do you know how much those things cost?"

I had some idea. After all, I grew up in the same hometown as the Unsers. It makes us all think we're experts.

"Oh, *yeah*," she continued. "Catherine thought Gil should just, like, write out a check. They had a terrible fight about it on the phone Friday night."

She gave a wistful look at the connecting door, closed now.

"You overheard the argument?"

"He was in the other room when the phone rang. We had just come in from dinner, about eight o'clock I guess, and I came in here to take off my shoes. Gil listened for awhile, and then I guess he just couldn't take it anymore. He let go with both barrels and really let her have it.

"I kind of went to a corner. I've never heard Gil lose it like that. I mean, he was really screaming. He told her if Jason didn't get off his ass and finish college and get a job, he'd never see a penny. He even went so far as to say that he was changing his will as soon as he got back to California. He would cut Jason off until he saw some effort on the kid's part."

"Pretty strong words," I observed. "Do you think Catherine might kill for her son?"

No hesitation. "I sure do. She may look like a helpless little thing, but she's as protective as a mama grizzly."

"What about Gil's dealings with Mack Garvey? Any trouble there?"

She had spread the crumpled tissue out now, flattening it against her tan leg with the palms of her hands.

"I only met Mack Garvey once. He seemed okay. But, Gil never talked about his business deals with me. They could have had problems, but I didn't know about them."

"What happened after the phone call?"

"Gil went out. He didn't invite me, so I turned on one of those pay-per-view movies on the TV. It wasn't very good, and

I drifted off to sleep before it was over. At some point, I must have switched off the set with the remote. I guess I was pretty tired."

"Weren't you worried about Gil when he didn't come back?"

"I didn't know he wasn't back at first. See, sometimes he preferred to sleep alone."

"Is that why you had two rooms?"

"That, and for phone calls. We'd know, by which phone was ringing, who the call was for. No slip-ups that way. And, Gil was a real workaholic. If he had business on his mind, he liked to bring his briefcase and all his paperwork into bed with him. He'd work on stuff until he couldn't keep his eyes open, then fall asleep with the whole mess stacked all around him. Sometimes, he'd wake up at five in the morning, pick up his pen, and start in, right where he'd left off."

He sounded like a thrilling bed partner to me.

"If he was in the mood for sex, he came to my room," she continued. "I didn't especially like it that way, him always calling the shots, but I learned early on not to complain."

I remembered the maid's description of Gil's violent temper.

Susan was obviously no Einstein, but she was pretty and energetic, and I had to wonder why she would stick with a guy like that. Maybe everyone has a price.

Maybe hers was a week in Hawaii now and then, and shopping trips to expensive boutiques.

"Anyway," she continued, "that morning I woke up early, and the connecting door was still closed, like I'd left it. I went down to exercise. When I came back, he was gone, but I didn't think too much about it. I went out to the pool, and figured he'd find me there. It wasn't unusual for him to go off by himself all day. I always played it by ear."

"Well, Susan, thanks for your help."

"Glad to. Charlie, I loved Gil."

Her voice cracked a little at this point. "I don't know anything about his business deals, but if Catherine Page had anything to do with this, I want to see her pay."

7

There was still one person I'd like to see today if possible. The mechanic, Joe Esposito. Mack had said that the police would probably be questioning him.

I needed to know what he told them.

First, though, a quick stop in my room was in order. I'd had a brainstorm of an idea. I really needed to talk to Jason Page. After the two versions of the story I'd just heard from Catherine and Susan, I felt Mack could see my justification in seeing Jason face to face.

It's too easy to hide one's true character over the phone. If I can look a guy in the eye, I can pick up a wealth of information behind the words.

I phoned down to the concierge and asked if he could check some flight times for me. I told him I'd like to leave early the next morning and return the same night or the morning after.

His voice oozed helpfulness, in hopes of a big tip, no doubt. He assured me he would have the information before the afternoon was out.

I hung up the phone, and my tired muscles turned longingly toward the bed. It stretched out warm, welcome promises of comfort to me, but it was still only three o'clock. If I stopped now, I might never get back up.

I had to try to find Joe Esposito.

Since Mack had cancelled the whole day's tours, I figured one of two things would happen. Mack might want Joe to use the extra time for some preventive maintenance on the aircraft, and therefore, he might be around the hangar. Or, Mack might have given Joe the day off, in which case tracking him down might be a real trick.

I wasn't exactly sure where the maintenance hangar was, but figured it had to be at the airport somewhere. It wasn't *that* big a place. If I drove around long enough, I could surely find it.

Once again, my snappy red convertible and I hit the road together. Up Rice Streeet, turn right, past the acres of tall sugar cane, eventually following the curved road past the helipads. I began scanning the area, driving as slowly as traffic would allow, hoping to spot the maintenance hangars.

Actually, it didn't turn out to be difficult at all. Just past the helipads sat a collection of buildings, ranging from the old to the decrepit, surrounded by a rust-brown chain link fence.

A white car with the words Kauai Police on the side, blue lights flashing on top, sat outside one of the buildings. It gave me a pretty good idea which place I was after.

I parked the tourist-mobile in the only empty space I could find, between a red pickup truck and a once-yellow Nissan station wagon that was more rust than paint. The pickup was hiked up about four extra feet off the ground by oversized tires which stuck way out on both sides, making the vehicle look like a gigantic roller skate.

I followed the perimeter of the chain link fence until I found a gate.

It was firmly closed, with a heavy-duty looking doorknob and there was a three-sided guard house just inside. The guard was nowhere to be seen, having apparently been lured by the excitement inside the strip of yellow crime scene tape surrounding the hangar. I did a sneaky little glance-around.

No one was near enough to be paying any attention to me. I wrapped my fingers around the hefty doorknob. It turned surprisingly smoothly. Shame, shame, guard person. Perhaps the recent lull in terrorist activity had made him lackadaisical.

Not one to question a good thing, I stepped through quickly and pushed the gate closed behind me. Lest I be caught lurking around the unguarded guard house, I walked quickly toward the hangar.

The building looked like an oversized World War II Quonset hut that had stood rusting to this spot since the day the Japs flew by. It had once been painted khaki green, now oxidized out to the flat gray color of lichen. The whole building looked like a great beached sperm whale.

Rust ate away at every seam in the corrugated metal. In places, it formed only a thin line, while in many spots it had already chewed through, leaving ragged gaps several inches big. I mentally gathered all my fingers and toes in close to my body, trying to remember when I'd had my last tetanus shot.

The double wide doors gaped fully open, and the nose of the helicopter peeked out at me, like an errant puppy sent to its kennel. The noise of wind and machinery outside made it impossible to hear anything of what was going on inside until I was practically touching the building. Voices came through, but distance blurred the words, making them indistinguishable.

Akito would not be pleased to see me, and I wished for the chance to spend a few minutes as a mouse in the corner before making my presence known. I tried to achieve this by slipping around the edge of the open door and standing very still with my back to the wall to scope out the situation.

The hangar was dark and relatively cool in comparison with the bright sun outside. I slipped my sunglasses into my purse and let my eyes adjust to the dim interior.

The helicopter sat in front of me and to my right. I could see dark blue pant legs with black policeman shoes on the far side of the ship. Its rear door stood open on that side, and I couldn't see an upper torso to go with the legs. Presumably, the officer was examining something inside.

A long workbench, littered with tools and mechanical looking things, stretched the length of the end wall on my left. Two red tool cabinets, the kind with wheels and about two dozen drawers each, stood against the back wall. Pegboard lined a large section of the wall over the workbench, which was hung with an assortment of belts, hoses, and metal things, like the automotive department of Wal-Mart. The air smelled of that garagey combination of grease, dust, and solvent.

Most of the activity, I noticed, centered in the rear corner of the hangar, to my left. Akito stood there, along with a short dark-complected man I didn't know. He wore navy blue shorts and a matching shirt with the tails hanging out. There was some kind of embroidered patch on his sleeve, and I assumed he was Joe, the mechanic.

The conversation looked pretty intense, but I couldn't catch the words. An aircraft part, a shaft of metal about two feet long, capped with a round connection at each end, lay on the floor near them. I didn't see anyone else around. I wanted to talk to Joe but debated the wisdom of butting in around Akito.

About that time, the other officer came around the nose of the helicopter and spotted me. Thankfully, it was not the same man I'd had the verbal exchange with at the station. He gave me a quizzical look, but didn't say anything. His movement caught Akito's eye.

"Hey! What's *she* doing here?" Akito's voice cut through the air, echoing off the high metal roof.

"I'm working for Mack Garvey," I told him, walking toward them. "I need to talk to his mechanic."

"How'd you get in here? Where's your airport security badge?"

I shrugged. "The gate was open, and no one stopped me." I hadn't seen any airport guard hanging around the crime scene tape, but what did I care if his butt was in the sling?

Akito didn't look any too happy about that. In fact, he looked like he wanted to kick somebody's ass; he just wasn't sure which one to start with.

Instead, he turned to the other officer. "We almost done here?" he growled.

The other man was a rather heavy-set local boy of about thirty-five. He handed Akito a plastic baggie with a bit of dust in it.

Vacuumings, I supposed, from the helicopter's interior.

Akito pointed to the metal object on the floor I had noticed earlier. "Wrap this, and take it in, too."

While the officer went out to the car to get something to wrap it in, I bent down to take a look at the object, careful not to touch it. I had no idea what the thing was, except that presumably it went somewhere on a helicopter. It looked like pretty solid metal, though. There was a good unmistakable blood stain near one end of it.

About ten feet away, a large spot on the greasy floor looked a bit murkier than the rest. Blood?

Looked to me like there was reason to believe we had our location and murder weapon.

I watched the young officer drape some plastic wrap over the metal object to protect fingerprints. He picked it up, and balanced one end against his leg while he neatly twisted the plastic around the opposite end. He repeated the procedure with the second end. His hands worked confidently, like he'd once worked as a sandwich wrapper at the deli.

"Heavy, huh?" I had noticed his biceps working to maneuver the long metal shaft.

Now that it was wrapped, he held it out to me. It weighed a good twenty pounds. More than I had expected, for sure. It would take a pretty good swing to heft this thing into the air and knock someone in the back of the head with it.

I handed it back to him before Akito caught me.

He was making one final snoop over the long workbench before taking his leave. Static crackled from his hand-held radio, and he murmured some response to it.

"Got everything?" he asked his partner.

The other man held up the weapon and his other baggies in response.

"Okay, Esposito, you can go on working. I guess we're finished." He gave me a dark look then motioned to his partner. He didn't speak to me and I was glad I didn't have to talk him into letting me stay awhile.

The mechanic had turned back to his workbench, ignoring me completely. In profile, I could see that his nose had been broken, probably more than once. The light from the fluorescent fixture over the bench played up the deep pits in his pockmarked face. His hair was about shoulder length, pulled back into a snarled rubber band.

"Are you Joe Esposito?" I asked, peeking around his shoulder.

He squirted some white grease out of a tube, like a shot of toothpaste, and rubbed it carefully with his index finger around the edge of a metal piece that might have been a small bearing of some sort. He fitted the greased part inside another, then wiped his finger against a filthy rag on the counter. The rag looked as if it could stand on its own.

"Hello?" I watched his face to see if a light came on. Nothing. "Look, Mack hired me to find out why he's accused of a murder he didn't commit. I'd just like to ask a couple of questions. Is that okay?"

I began to wonder if the man was deaf, but he finally turned to look at me. He had droop-cornered dark eyes that some women might find attractive in the bedroom. Here, the effect was anything but sexy. I stepped back half a pace.

"You work for Mack, don't you?" I asked. "Don't you care whether he goes to jail or not?"

He shrugged. Apparently, the prospect of jail wasn't the worst thing he could think of. His stubborn silence was really beginning to irritate me though. I could feel my hands starting to clench up.

"Listen, jerk, even if you don't give a damn about Mack, don't you care whether you have a job next week?" I can't help it. Obliquity in others tends to bring out strong reactions in me.

He spun on me so quickly, I thought he was going to grab me by my shirt collar. I jumped back about twelve inches.

"Look, lady, you don't know nothin'. You a stranger here, and you come buttin' you nose in where you know nothin'. Mack, he so far in debt, I don't know if my next paycheck gonna bounce anyway."

He jabbed the greasy index finger toward my nose. "For all I know, maybe he did kill that guy. He sure sounded like he might. But it really piss me off when the cops think I help him, cause I didn't. I got nothin' to do with this."

His brown skin had a dangerous red undertone to it. I was tempted to back my way out the door, but something he said had just sunk in.

"Wait a minute," I ventured cautiously. "You say Mack *sounded* like he wanted to kill the guy? Did they have a fight?"

He puffed a sharp breath out his nose. "Right here in this hangar Friday night."

He gathered up a couple of screwdrivers and several wrenches from the workbench, and carried them to the red tool chests. I followed at his heels, like a kid wanting candy.

"So, you were here? You heard them?" Mack had told me that Joe never showed Friday night. He said he had gone back to the office and had chicken for dinner.

He never mentioned Gil Page being here.

Joe made another trip to the workbench. He picked through small items on the bench, sorting out nuts, bolts, fuses, and screws before he answered. He put each of the items into special drawers in a little cabinet.

"I work til 'bout nine-thirty, ten Friday night, then I take a break for dinner. I gotta finish some work on the ship, then Mack gonna come later, and we do tracking. I get back from my dinner break, walk up to the door, hear Mack and this other guy screaming at each other. Sounds like they ready to tear each other apart. I don't wanna be in the middle. I drive around awhile, come back 'bout half hour later. They both gone, I figure okay, I do my work."

"They were gone when you came back? What about that... that metal thing the police took away? Was that here?"

"Police find that on the floor under the workbench. It's usually on the shelf over there. Old spare hydraulic servo."

"And you told the police about the fight, I suppose."

He didn't respond. He pulled a key ring off his belt, and locked the red cabinets.

"Did they tell you they think you helped Mack dump the body?"

"I told you, I got nothin' to do with this."

He grabbed a baseball cap from where it hung on a nail, and pulled it on. "Better get outta here," he said, "I'm locking up."

I stood aside as he pulled the two heavy doors shut, and padlocked them. The yellow police tape was gone now. Apparently, Akito felt they had thoroughly investigated the scene.

The afternoon sun had sunk below the mountains, and the parking lot was bathed in pinkish light. Since Joe and I were both heading for the gate, we ended up walking together. The female guard was in her little wooden structure when we passed. She rose from her seat, and I thought she was going to question me, but Joe reached for the gate's doorknob and opened it. I walked through without a word to the guard.

Catherine Page was standing in the parking lot. She wore white linen slacks and a white cotton sweater that made her look cool and clean, too clean to be standing in the red dirt lot. Her hair was freshly done, her tapered nails now polished pale apricot.

"I was hoping to catch Mack Garvey," she told me.

"He's not here. Joe just locked up the hangar."

She carefully kept her eyes on me, avoiding any direct glance at Joe, just as he was avoiding looking at her. Here among the shabby buildings and rusted cars, she was like a sweet angel in white. I couldn't imagine any male not wanting to gaze upon her, at least for a minute.

I got the distinct feeling an undercurrent had just rippled through the lot.

Joe got into the beefed-up red pickup truck next to my rental and started it with a rumble. Catherine and I stepped to one side as he backed the clumsy contraption out of its space. As he pulled away, I saw him watching us in his rearview mirror.

I turned to Catherine and noticed she was staring through the fence at the hangar.

"Is that where it happened?" Her voice went high and thin.

I nodded. I couldn't think of anything appropriate to say.

"You know," she said sweetly, "I don't think I ever hated anyone in my life the way I hated Gil."

It took a moment for the words to reach me, coming as they did past her angel exterior. I caught myself staring at her.

I didn't really need to ask why she felt that way.

Already, she had lost a little of the beaten-puppy look I'd noticed earlier. I tried to picture her wielding twenty pounds of greasy hydraulic servo, but it didn't quite gel.

On the other hand, she'd certainly managed to get here almost immediately after the body had been discovered. It was entirely possible that she and Joe were in this together. I better check out the Friday night phone call and the airline schedules.

She had turned to stare again at the hangar.

"The worst part was having to watch him abuse Jason," she said.

"Physical abuse?" I wondered how a mother could sit back and watch.

I wasn't sure whether she heard me. She seemed wrapped in a private world. Her eyes were narrowed, her thoughts turned inward.

Her voice, when it came, was merely a whisper. "I'm so glad he's gone," she said.

If she killed him, I decided, she did it for her own survival.

I murmured an apology about needing to be somewhere and got into my car. As I pulled onto the highway, the light was fading fast and so were my eyelids. I let the valet park my car and dragged my feet through the lobby toward the elevators.

"Miss Parker!"

I turned to see the concierge. He was a sandy little man, thirty-something, about five-six, his thinning hair cut close all around. He introduced himself as Morton Willis. His braid-trimmed uniform was crisp and unwrinkled. My own linen suit had wilted hours earlier.

His manner was as ingratiating in person as it had been over the phone.

"I was able to get you on the six o'clock flight to San Francisco in the morning. I hope it was all right to book the seat; they said it was the only one available for two days."

I'd forgotten all about our conversation. Was it only a few hours ago?

Fatigue was making my muscles Jello-like, but I had no choice. I couldn't wait another two days to talk to Jason Page. I took the ticket folder he extended toward me. I handed him a twenty dollar tip.

"Oh, Morton, one other question." I might as well get my money's worth out of the guy.

"Yes, Miss Parker?"

"I need to know if Susan Turner requested a pay-per-view movie Friday night."

He wanted to tell me something about the hotel's assuring its guests privacy, but the twenty dollar bill still rested crisply in his hand.

"It's official," I said. "If I don't find out, I'm sure the police will ask."

Without another word, he turned toward the registration desk. I followed, feeling like a kid at Baskin Robbins begging for a small taste. He stepped behind the desk, and signed on to one of the computer terminals. His fingers skipped over the keys, pausing now and then for the next screen to come up.

"Yes," he said, finally. "Ten p.m. Friday, *The Curse of Dracula*."

Hmm, Susan didn't seem like the Dracula type. I thanked him as he quickly signed off the terminal.

"Shall I arrange a wake-up call for five in the morning?"

"Sure. Five." Ugh. These early mornings were becoming a habit.

I sank against the back of the elevator for the ride up.

A couple got on at the fourth floor, probably bound for the restaurant on twelve. She wore a strapless print dress of bright orange hibiscus and green leaves which hit her about three inches below the buns, and would probably require a paint scraper to remove. Her date was giving it a good try though, right there in the elevator. I wondered if they would make it through dinner before making a hasty retreat to their room. I got off on seven, giving them five whole floors for a quickie.

My message light was blinking again. Drake. He wanted to know if I'd eaten dinner yet. I couldn't remember.

"Let me take you out," he begged.

"Honestly, Drake, I'm beat. I'm heading for the tub right now."

"Let me join you."

Even in my weakened condition the idea was powerfully attractive. Something held me back, though. Our first time, if there was to be a first time, should be special.

I filled him in on my plan to fly to San Francisco.

"Tell you what, why don't you pick me up when I get back?"

I pulled the ticket out and looked at it. My return flight left San Francisco late afternoon. *If* the airline was on sched-ule, I should arrive back on Kauai about ten p.m. the next night. He said he would be there.

I peeled clothes off as I made my way to the bathroom. I poured half of the little freebie bottle of bubble bath under the rushing tap then went back into the bedroom to get organized. I hate being disorganized, and I hate things messy. At home, I can almost tell if someone has walked through my living room because some little thing will be out of place.

I picked up the dirty clothes I had just taken off, and stuffed them into a laundry bag. I'd leave them to be done tomorrow while I was gone. I pulled out a small collapsible carry-on bag I take along whenever I travel somewhere that I'm likely to overdo the shopping. I had no plans of staying over in San Francisco, but it never hurt to be ready.

I would wear my generic black slacks and my new cotton batik print blouse. In case of an emergency stay-over, I stuck a change of underwear and a clean shirt into the small bag. In the morning, I'd add my make-up bag and a hairbrush.

My inflatable neck pillow and cassette stereo would help tune out all extraneous noises. I'd try to sleep on the plane, so I could be awake by the time I got back to Drake.

Fluffs of bubbles rose a foot above the edge of the tub like meringue on a lemon pie. Perhaps half the bottle had been a bit much. I turned the cold water completely off, leaving the hot at a trickle. There's nothing worse than a bath that begins to cool down before I'm satiated.

My tired muscles loved it as I settled them down into the steaming water. I leaned my neck back against the end of the tub and let the water lull me. Soon, I felt my eyelids drooping; I knew I'd better get out before I ended up spending the night under water.

The clock at my bedside told me it was eight o'clock, but I guess my body was still on mainland time. I set the alarm, just in case the wake-up call didn't come through.

I must have died the very minute my head hit the pillow, because the next thing I was aware of was the ringing telephone. I wanted to punch the cheery good-morning person in the face, which is probably why they don't deliver wake-up calls in person.

It was still dark out, and my brain wasn't in gear yet. I am not a quick riser. My already-packed bag waited near the door. I brushed my teeth and splashed some water on my face, consciously trying not to come fully awake just yet. I tossed the last two items into my bag and called the front desk to get me a cab.

By the time I stumbled downstairs, the car was waiting to deliver me to the airport, where I managed to find my flight. It was direct, so I snagged a pillow and blanket before they were all gone and tucked myself in.

Nestled against the window, my Walkman pouring Barry Manilow into my ears, I slept through the announcements, breakfast, and whatever other courtesies they may have tried to foist upon me.

I awoke four hours later feeling like a new person. I could have used the bathroom, but it seemed like too much bother to squeeze past the teenage boy who must have been about six foot seven, judging by the length of his legs, just to get into a lavatory smaller than a phone booth. I did a little stretch in place and accepted the flight attendant's offer of a hot wash cloth and a cup of coffee.

I could now face the world.

In the ladies room at San Francisco International, I pulled out my little zippered makeup bag for a quick fixup. Even under the best of conditions, I don't take a lot of time at this ritual. Foundation, blush, and lipstick are about all I ever mess with.

A woman approached the mirror beside me, and settled her carry-on bag on the counter with a thump. Out came two zippered cosmetic cases. I tried to look busy, but I have to confess, I was probably staring. She gazed intently at her own face, inspecting each square centimeter, and paid no attention whatever to me. I thought she looked fine already, and I was curious to see just what improvements she would deem necessary.

She first went to work on her eyes, applying concealer from a greasy-looking stick to the skin below them. Next came eye shadow, three colors in all, which she placed with extreme precision to different sections of the lids. Once the colors were in place, she took a Q-Tip and smudged them together, making the original colors blend into one. I didn't understand why she hadn't just bought that color in the first place, but I guess some things are beyond my realm.

Liner pencil came next, two colors applied, blended into one. She finished with two coats of mascara to each set of lashes, then rechecked the job, dabbing with a clean Q-Tip whenever she found minuscule errors. By this time I was openly staring.

Now, she pulled out a bottle of liquid foundation and proceeded to dot the contents all over her face. With a small wedge of sponge, she spread the dots together, leaning close to the mirror to be sure she hadn't missed a spot. I was fascinated by the variety of jars, tubes and implements that appeared from the two cases. My bathroom at home isn't this well stocked.

I could see that the routine would go on for some time yet, and I had long ago run out of things to do to myself. I ran a quick brush through my hair and figured I was as ready as I'd ever be. I left the other woman at the mirror, sweeping blusher onto her cheekbones with a long-handled brush. A litter of cotton swabs and tissues had begun to collect on the counter.

Catherine Page had given me phone numbers for their home and Jason's friend, but no addresses. I hadn't wanted to tell her I was planning to visit her son in person, lest she feel the need to brief him first. I stopped at a pay phone and looked in the book for the Page's address.

Gilbert Page Enterprises was listed with a downtown address, but no personal listing. I realized that Mill Valley probably had its own directory.

There were lots of Cramers in the book, and I finally found one whose number matched the one Catherine had given me for Jason's friend. I copied the address into my little spiral.

At the rental car desk a helpful young junior executive type, with a crisp white shirt and company logo tie, gave me a couple of maps, on which he drew arrows in pen showing me where I needed to go.

"Ever heard of a health club called Workout Heaven?" I asked him. "It must be new, it's not in the book."

He chewed his lip a minute. "I drive by something like that coming to work," he said. "I can't think exactly where, but I know I've seen their sign."

He pulled the map back and turned it to face himself. "Somewhere here along Bayshore Boulevard, I think." He ran the pen back and forth along a two or three block stretch.

I told him I'd find it, then flashed him what I hoped was a very grateful smile.

Out in the lot, I located my rental car and sat inside letting it warm up while I studied the map. I pulled my lightweight jacket out of my carry-on bag. I'd forgotten how chilly San Francisco always feels.

Bayshore Boulevard was on my way into the city, with Mill Valley beyond that, so I figured I'd hit Susan's place first.

Mark Cramer's address was in the city, south of Market Street. That would be my second stop.

I started watching too late and realized I'd already passed the stretch of Bayshore my friend had indicated on the map. Buildings were thinning out, so I decided I better turn around. I found a place to do it and doubled back.

Sure enough, heading this direction, the sign was easy to spot on my right.

I pulled off, getting out of the traffic, before I realized that the sign said "Future Home of Workout Heaven."

I was facing a big flat dirt lot, empty except for a bulldozer and three pickup trucks with Hayes Construction Co. signs on their sides. I looked around, making sure I was in the right place. Looked like Workout Heaven was still quite a way into the future.

The air was nippy as I got out of the car, and I zipped my jacket up all the way. The salty breeze off the bay whipped my hair across my face like a Middle Eastern veil.

It looked like the bulldozer was about done with its work. The ground was all nicely leveled. Four men were in various stages of measuring and driving stakes into the ground.

One guy in a red hard hat seemed to be in charge. I headed toward him.

The foreman had pale hair which curled up around the edges of his hard hat, and his face was so wind burned it looked like it had been scoured with cleanser, giving him an inexpensive dermabrasion treatment. He was shorter than I, about five-four, I'd guess, with a barrel chest and a belly that hung generously over his belt buckle. His jeans seemed in imminent danger of slipping off his almost non-existent butt.

"Hi," I said. "Is this Susan Turner's place?" I tried to muster a smile, but my hair whipped across my face and stuck to the fronts of my teeth.

He was fighting his own private battle with a set of plans that were refusing to stay unrolled in the brisk wind. He looked flustered and irritated.

"Yeah," he growled, giving up and letting the plans have their own way. "Where is she, anyway? I got all the dirt work done here; the guy's waiting to be paid."

He waved toward the bulldozer operator.

"My own crew's been on the job all week, payday's Friday, and do I have her deposit check yet?" He opened the door of his pickup truck, and jammed the unruly plans inside, slamming the door to keep the disobedient critters inside.

"I *knew* better than to trust that lady," he muttered. "She don't know nothin about how business works."

I thought it rather unprofessional of him to be telling me all this. For all he knew, I might be someone snooping into Susan's private business. Since, of course, I was, I didn't mention this little blunder on his part.

"I think she's been out of town," I ventured.

"Shit! That's it! Not one more lick of work here until I get money from that broad."

He put two fingers between his teeth and let out a whistle that almost deafened me.

"Quittin' time," he shouted toward the other men.

Without a word among them, they dropped the wooden stakes right where they were and headed for their trucks. He hopped into his truck, too, and waved me a little salute.

Within ninety seconds, I was completely alone, standing in the flat dirt lot.

I was happy enough to be out of the wind as I got back into the rental car, but felt frustrated by the conversation's abrupt end. I stared at the empty dirt lot for a good four or five minutes, wishing I'd had a chance to ask the contractor a few more questions.

How did this jibe with Susan's version of her busy health club?

Had she actually described it as bustling with customers working out with weights, jumping around in unison aerobically? Or, had she merely conveyed that impression? I know she'd invited me to come by and work out anytime I was in town. I tried to picture myself in the classes.

The dance aerobics might be fun, but my childhood dream of becoming a Rockette had given way years ago. Face it, I have all the grace and precision of a goony bird. The years of defending myself against my brothers gave me more muscle than elegance. My little fantasy, therefore, is still a secret.

The blowing dust and sea spray had coated my windshield with a thin opaque film, and I had to search for the washers before I trusted myself out on the road again.

Locating Mark Cramer's address proved more difficult than I had anticipated. The street was shown on my map as being only a block or two south of Market, but it turned out to be one of those that dead-ends periodically then starts again somewhere else, continuing in little segments for twenty or thirty blocks.

I managed to find the correct little segment on my third try.

To say that the neighborhood was run-down would have been complimentary. The four houses facing the half-block long street were probably of Victorian ancestry, but certainly not from the same set of genes as their Nob Hill neighbors.

One or two old trees, tall and beaten by time, were about all that remained of any landscaping that once might have been. Weeds outnumbered shrubs by at least a thousand to one, and the former lawns had long since become hard packed dirt, beaten down by children's feet, motorcycles, and parked cars.

Judging by the number of cars parked along the short street, most if not all of the homes had been converted to apartments. I wondered about a kid from Jason's background finding a best friend here. I wondered what Catherine Page thought of it, if she knew.

There was no place left to park on the street, so I pulled into the driveway of the Cramer residence.

The house had once been yellow with white Victorian gingerbread trim. The yellow had now faded out to the shade of mayonnaise gone bad, while all that remained of the white paint were flaky chunks here and there. The exposed wood beneath had rotted beyond the help of any sanding and painting repair job. The building's entire structural integrity looked questionable.

A refrigerator sat on the screened front porch. A large metal hasp and padlock on it made me wonder if the appliance worked. Was the lock there to keep kids out, or food in? Or both?

The driveway ran in two narrow concrete tracks beside the house, clear to the back yard where a separate garage building stood with doors open wide. I decided to try that first.

The garage was in somewhat better repair than the house. A car was parked inside, facing outward. Its hood had been removed, towels draped over the front grill and the left and right quarter panels like surgical cloths. Its engine was apparently the object of the procedure. Two young men bent over it, their concentration complete.

"Three-eighths." I heard one of them say to the other.

The second guy slapped a wrench into the requester's hand.

"Naw, open-end."

The wrench was exchanged for another. About this time, they noticed me and glanced up. I half expected them to be wearing surgical masks.

"Jason Page?" I asked.

I knew immediately which one he was. He had so much of Catherine in him, there could be no doubt. His build was slight, although his arms appeared well-muscled under the one-piece white coveralls he wore. He had Catherine's brown hair and eyes, and her delicate mouth. As far as I could tell, he bore no resemblance to his father. No wonder he was mother's little darling.

He took half a step toward me, but made no move to shake hands. Looking at the grease encrusted palms, I decided it was all right. I could pass on formalities.

"I'm Charlie Parker," I said, handing him my card. "I'm looking into your father's death."

He shrugged. "What about it?"

I watched for the complex signs of emotion that must go with a young man's losing his father in a violent manner.

I could see none.

I knew he was closer to his mother, but surely he felt *something*.

"Are you doing okay, Jason?"

He looked at the card again. "You an investigator or a shrink?"

He shoved the card into the pocket of his coveralls and turned back to the car. His friend had found something important to do at the back of the garage.

"Okay, Jason, you're right. That part of it may not matter. We can stick to the facts if you want to. Where were you last Friday night?"

"Home, I guess."

"Your mother says you weren't."

"Okay, then I was here. Whenever I'm not home, I'm here. You can ask Mark if you want to."

Mark glanced up and nodded. Jason proceeded to wrench something on the car's engine. I wasn't getting much out of him.

I walked around to the side of the car. I thought it had once been a Chevy, although I couldn't swear to it now. The rear was painted hot pink, which blended into fluorescent yellow somewhere in the middle. The sides were plastered with stickers from different brands of oil, tires, spark plugs, and filters.

"These all your sponsors?" I asked.

"Some of 'em give us a little cash. Most of 'em just give us the stickers," Jason told me.

"Expensive hobby, I guess."

"Yeah," he said, "I guess so. We really want to get into the big leagues, though. The NASCAR circuit. My mom was trying to talk Dad into giving me enough money to get a good car. This thing's okay, but it's small time."

I stuck my head in the side window. The doors had been welded shut and the interior completely stripped, empty except for one bucket seat with massive shoulder and lap belts for the driver. Everything inside the car, including the roll cage of heavy pipe, was painted black. I noticed a small cylinder, about the size of a home fire extinguisher.

"What's that?" I asked.

Jason came up beside me to see what I was talking about.

"Oh, nitrous," he said. "If I need a little extra hit, I flip this switch." He pointed to a small toggle switch on the console. "Whhommm!" He skidded the palms of his two hands together, shooting one way out front. I got the picture.

"Neat," I said. "I hadn't heard of that before."

"Yeah, lots of guys use it now. Mostly in the better cars, though. We have a pretty good advantage in our class with this one."

He was warming up to me a bit now, so I decided to press my advantage.

"You really were hoping your dad could help you get a better car, weren't you?"

"Well, geez, it just seems so unfair, ya know? I mean, my dad does okay, but he's not rich, ya know? I mean, he doesn't have a half mil to hand out to everyone who asks. But, he manages to give money to that helicopter guy. He manages to give money to that girlfriend of his. Why can't he give his own kid some? I got dreams, too. I got plans."

He turned quickly back to the engine, hiding his face from me for a few seconds. I couldn't think of an answer for him. He was still at an age where his wants would take precedence over anything else. The business sense of a deal wouldn't make any difference to him. He just wasn't old enough yet to see that a race car would never earn back the investment.

"What about your mom, Jason? How does she see it?"

"Mom's okay," he said. His face lost a lot of its tightness when he spoke of Catherine. "She goes to bat for me whenever she can."

"Did she and your father argue about the car?"

"That, and everything else," he said. "Everybody argued with Dad. He wasn't open to any idea that wasn't his. If you didn't go along with his way of doing things, you got screamed at. Sometimes Mom would fight back. Usually, it was just easier to fix herself a drink and keep quiet."

"How did you cope with that?" My own parents had fought a lot when I was a kid, but it was all verbal, and never directed at us kids. Somehow I just let it roll off me. I was curious how Jason had handled it all.

"Me? I'd just get out. I'd come over here, and work on the car with Mark. Mark's dad skipped out a long time ago, so there's only his mom here. She's cool. She comes out to watch us race sometimes."

"You have any idea who might have killed him?"

"Yeah, about two dozen I could name off the top of my head who hated him bad enough, including Mom and me. But, to actually pick up the gun and do it? Who knows?" He shrugged, then turned to look straight at me. "Charlie, do you think I'll ever get my car now?"

I couldn't answer that. I thanked him, and walked back to my car.

Jason Page was clearly too wrapped up in himself to have planned and carried out a murder. Even if he'd seriously thought of it, which I doubted, he would have decided it was too much work. I could see, though, how he would have thrown enough logic into his arguments to bring Catherine around to his side.

I inserted the ignition key and cranked life into the rental. When I glanced up before putting it into reverse, I saw that Mark had walked over to Jason's side and put his arm around his friend's shoulders.

I started to raise my fingers to wave goodbye, but realized they weren't looking at me. As I put the car in gear, Mark leaned forward and gave Jason a kiss, on the mouth.

So much for Catherine's little fantasy about her son and the girl next door.

8

I drove away thinking about Jason and Mark, wondering whether Gil Page had guessed his son's secret. I couldn't picture a man like Gil being very understanding about it. The conflicts between them must have been endless.

Maybe I shouldn't write Jason off as a suspect quite so quickly.

The phone directory had listed Gilbert Page Enterprises at a downtown address. It wasn't far if I hit Van Ness Avenue. I decided to buzz by there even though nothing so far in the case had brought his San Francisco business into the picture. You just never know.

Traffic was pleasantly light. I wasn't sure why. Maybe I had hit a temporary lull between the lunch rush and the go-home rush.

I found the building easily enough, but getting a parking space was another story. On my third trip around, a spot opened up on a side street two blocks over.

Thankfully, it wasn't one of San Francisco's steeper streets, but it was bad enough. Parallel parking, especially on an incline, has never been one of my strong suits. It took me two tries to get reasonably close to the curb. Beyond that, I wasn't willing to endure the embarrassment. I felt sure dozens of people must be watching me from their office windows.

I turned my wheels into the curb, hoping I remembered which way was correct. My armpits felt damp by the time I climbed out.

The wind was still brisk here in town, but less chilly than it had been at the construction site. A wadded up brown lunch sack rolled past me, an empty soda can trailing close behind. I was glad I hadn't worn a skirt.

The sun felt weak, screened from its full effectiveness by a high, thin cloud layer. On Van Ness horns tooted and exhaust fumes permeated the air. I glanced around as I locked the car, getting my bearings.

Page's address was listed on McAllister, and I found it just down from the State Office Building. It was an imposing place. The plate glass entry doors must have been a good inch thick with brass handles I had a hard time getting my hand around.

My heels clacked across the marble lobby, heading for the office directory near the elevators. I was curious to see how much of the building his business occupied.

Gilbert Page Enterprises was listed in suite 500. There were no other listings on the fifth floor. If indeed his offices encompassed the entire floor, I was prepared to be impressed. The elevator doors slid open, then closed with a whisper behind me. I pressed five and stood with my arms folded awkwardly. Left alone in the elevator, I wasn't quite sure what to do with myself. When others are present, you can always stare up at the floor numbers. But, what do you do alone? I didn't have to worry about it long.

The doors whooshed open at five, discharging me into a wide hallway carpeted in deep blue. The walls were pale gray, hung with pastel watercolors of northern California seascapes. The hall formed a T just beyond the elevators. Suite 500 was marked conspicuously on the first door I came to.

Out of curiosity, I walked the length of the hall to my right, scanning the doors. The other suites were numbered, but none had a company name listed. I tried the door on 504. It was locked. I wasn't sure what significance that held.

The door to Page's offices slid open on well-oiled hinges. I found myself in a large reception area, facing an empty desk. The carpeting was the same deep blue as the hall outside, the walls the same pale gray, as if the entire floor had been decorated to please the tenant of this suite.

There was a conference room to my left, behind a glass wall. The lights were off, the chairs neatly placed around a spotless smoked glass table.

The furniture was quality. The reception desk was cherry, solid and elegant. The matching credenza held two bronze statuettes. I'd seen them once at a San Francisco gallery. The limited edition introductory price had been seventy-five hundred each.

A sofa/loveseat grouping upholstered in a softly patterned blue, gray, and burgundy silk stood in the corner in case I might want to be comfortable while I waited.

To my right was a closed door with a brass name plate, Gilbert Page.

Behind the receptionist's desk were closed double doors, leading presumably to the chambers where the peons slaved away. I cleared my throat a couple of times, figuring that was fair warning to anyone who cared to come checking on me. No one did, so I casually approached the desk.

It's really not smart to leave me unattended in places like this. I tend to get nosy.

As nonchalantly as possible, I did a visual sweep of the room. I didn't spot any surveillance equipment, no silent human observers. I assumed there must be a buzzer of some kind in the back that would be activated when the front door opened.

Someone would surely come through those double doors at any second.

I kept my ears tuned for the sound of the doorknob turning while I let my eyes wander over the desk top. Although it was scrupulously neat, little clues indicated that the receptionist was something more than merely a telephone answerer. A green columnar pad revealed (when I happened to lift the cover) neat rows of figures.

The account names were cryptically referred to, with names such as Group 4 and Venture Holdings. That didn't tell me much.

She hadn't reached the bottom line yet, but was far enough along that some quick math in my head told me the ink on the bottom line would be red. The rest of the work in progress consisted of two manilla folders of bills, PAID and TO BE PAID. The latter was thicker.

I still had not heard a sound, other than the neutral hum of the air conditioning.

I was half tempted to plop myself down in her chair and start on the desk drawers, but figured that really would be going too far. I was dying to see what lay beyond Gilbert Page's private office door. Even entertained the idea of closing myself in there for the rest of the day, hoping not to get caught. My luck though, I'd need to go to the bathroom, and I'd be trapped, waiting for closing time with my legs crossed.

Without being blatant, in the five minutes I'd been there I'd seen about all there was to see. Where was everyone?

I finally decided to risk facing whatever lay beyond the double doors. I tapped with my right hand, in a gesture that was more form than substance, while I turned the knob with my left. The door opened into a narrow hall running perpendicular to me.

Straight ahead was a blank gray wall. To the left were rest rooms. Generic symbols on the closed doors defined his and hers. To my right, the blue carpet continued for about ten feet, then abruptly ended.

What I could see beyond the end of the carpet looked like unfinished construction. The concrete floor was spattered with paint spots and gobs of drywall paste. Bare two-by-four studs framed the far wall, which was covered on the opposite side by drywall but lay exposed on the inside. Ribbons of variously colored wire ran through holes in the studs to metal outlet boxes, ending in tangles. I tiptoed to the end of the carpet and peeked around the corner.

The gray wall which formed the narrow hall was nothing but a facade. Beyond was an empty room, probably fifty feet square.

Bare metal I-beams formed the ceiling, with silver heating and cooling ductwork suspended below. A paint-flecked metal step ladder stood in the middle of the cavernous expanse. Five-gallon cans, three of them, were lined up against the far wall. There were a few odd scraps of lumber strewn around the floor, certainly not enough to finish the job.

I stared, trying to assimilate what I was seeing. No wonder Page kept everyone in the dark about his business activities. The whole thing was a fake.

Just then, I heard a toilet flush.

My heart immediately switched to staccato. I had begun to believe I was alone. I peered back into the fake hall. The sound of water running came from behind the doors to the girl's room. I dashed for the double doors, jerking the left one open as quickly as the pneumatic closer would allow.

Had the water stopped? I couldn't tell.

I practically leaped around the corner of the reception desk, and crossed the room in about three bounds. I was seated on the sofa, legs crossed, magazine in hand, when the door opened. I looked down at my shirt to see if my heart was thudding visibly. It certainly was making a terrible racket.

"Oh, my goodness, you startled me!" She laid her hand across her chest. That was some consolation in my state of near-cardiac arrest.

Gil's receptionist was in her mid-thirties, a petite five-two, her frosted blond hair cut chin length, and carefully arranged to suggest that she had just stepped in out of the wind.

The few extra pounds she carried around the middle were expertly concealed beneath her tailored blue suit. Nude, she would probably be soft as a tub of whipped butter, but the strong lines of the suit trimmed her right down.

She wore a matching blue blouse with a bow at the neck, and blue-dyed snakeskin pumps. I wondered whether she had carried a swatch of the office carpet with her when she shopped for the outfit. It was a perfect match. A hint of lemon air freshener wafted through the doorway with her.

I checked out her jewelry. Her watch was either a Rolex or a damn good copy. No wedding band. That explained how she found the money for her clothing budget.

"Has anyone helped you yet?" she inquired.

Fat chance. I guess I was supposed to believe that a cast of hundreds awaited their cues behind the closed doors. Okay, I could play her silly game.

"Actually, I came to see Mr. Page. Is he in?"

"No, I'm afraid he's out of town at the moment."

Well, that was sure the truth.

She had taken her seat behind the desk, and began to straighten the already neat folders. Her movements were quick and efficient, designed to accomplish maximum effect with minimum effort. She was not good at making busywork.

"May I inquire about the nature of your business? Perhaps someone else might help you."

I could practically see them lining up in the hall.

"Well, maybe. I'm looking for office space in this area and heard he might have something for lease."

"Office space? Where would you have heard that?"

I fumbled for an answer. I don't mind lying, but I really hate to get caught at it.

"Mr. Page is in the equipment leasing business. We don't have any real estate dealings at all."

"Oh, *equipment* leasing," I said, pulling myself out of the soft sofa cushions with difficulty. "I must have got my wires crossed. I could have sworn someone told me he had offices for lease. What sort of equipment do you lease?"

She held me with a level gaze that said she knew my story was pure bullshit. At least she had the good grace not to say so.

"Computers, office machines, that sort of thing," she said flatly.

"Oh, good," I plowed ahead. "Maybe I'll contact you again once I get my office space. I'll probably need some equipment." I tried to come up with a sincere smile, but it felt weak. I edged my way to the door.

She smiled fixedly. I wondered what she thought I was up to. Probably a bill collector or process server trying to get at Page. She could have gotten rid of me much more efficiently by just saying that he was dead.

I didn't breathe normally again until I was back on the street. The two block walk to my car proved beneficial in getting my tangled thoughts in some kind of order. I remembered reading something about an equipment leasing scam a couple of years ago. What had it been about?

It was a limited partnership, I thought, as the story came back to me, set up to provide tax shelters to people who made so much money they couldn't figure out what do to with it all. Turned out the IRS disallowed the shelter, so the investors lost the deductions they thought they were getting.

To top it off, the partnership declared one small dividend, then filed Chapter 7. Three hundred investors lost fifty thou each. I never heard any satisfactory explanation of where the fifteen million ended up.

My former fiancé, Brad North, was the only person I knew dumb enough to get into it. And he's a lawyer. Kinda makes you think.

Had Gilbert Page set up a similar scam? Were they just about to enter the bankruptcy phase of the game?

It could explain the operating losses that showed on the books. It could also give several hundred more people a reason to kill him.

I unlocked the car door and stepped in, glad to be out of the persistent wind. I was a little at a loss for what to do next. My watch told me it was three o'clock, but I honestly couldn't remember whether I'd changed it. I could still be on Hawaiian time. The sun was hazy behind the high cloud layer, though, and it felt like mid-afternoon.

I suddenly realized I was starving. The thought of driving up to North Beach, and finding a pizzeria was tempting, but I figured I better head the other way. By the time I turned in the rental car, and checked in at the airport, I'd just about have time for something to eat there before my flight. Airport food couldn't compare remotely with anything I'd find in North Beach, but, oh well. Another time.

I found myself thinking of Drake as I anticipated my flight. I turned in the rental car, shouldered my small carry-on bag, and thought of Drake. I presented my ticket, stood in line, and inched my way toward my seat.

A handsome male flight attendant offered drinks. For an instant, some trick of light made me think he was Drake. My heart surprised me by doing a momentary little dance.

I'm a pretty independent person and not unaccustomed to traveling alone. But, I found it comforting to think that he'd be there to meet me this time. I drifted into a pleasant sleep thinking about him, and awoke from a series of weird dreams about an Oriental police officer driving a race car with a blond exercise instructor at his side.

It was pitch dark outside.

9

Sex with Drake made me euphoric — mellow inside yet almost super-charged at the same time. His mouth caused me to melt. His hands knew all the right places to touch. I found it easy to give myself over to him in a way I had never done with anyone before.

It had been too long since my last relationship. Two years since the six month stint with Edward, the dreamy eyed man with wispy blond hair who fancied himself a poet. His lines of verse had enchanted me in the beginning, but I came to see them as meaningless bunches of words he had dredged up from somewhere in the bottom of a bottle of Stoli. That's probably where his sex drive came from, too, because it was the only time he was ever in the mood.

It ended with Edward slowly yet abruptly, as I suppose many relationships do. I had long since lost my fervor over his poetry. I had quit spending the night, because waking up next to his vodka-laden breath turned my stomach. I was looking for a way to end it gently.

The night he confided to me that he was bi-sexual seemed like the perfect time.

I incinerated the toothbrush and spare changes of clothing he used to leave at my house. I had myself tested for HIV, although he swore he had not been with a man in three years. Perhaps my behavior was a bit unfeeling, but truthfully, I felt stupid for not having found this out ahead of time.

Thankfully, I tested okay, but it put the fear of God in me. I was only now starting to get in the mood again.

Drake Langston came along at just the right time. He'd been married for fifteen years, up until a year ago. His emotions, like mine, were just beginning to heal.

The fact that I was here on vacation kept us from getting too serious. The seriousness of the situation kept us from taking each other too lightly. I wasn't interested in one night stands, but I wasn't ready for a full-fledged commitment, either. I sensed the same feelings in Drake.

We'd take it easy and see what happened.

The hotel room lay in gray shadow, the furnishings colorless in the dim light filtering around the edge of the drape. I stretched sensuously, my body remembering last night's emotions.

Drake lay asleep on his side, his face free of the past few day's stresses. I reached toward him and, sensing my nearness, he rolled to his back and pulled me toward him. I nestled into his shoulder. I loved his scent, warm with sleep.

"Awake already?" he mumbled. He stroked my hair as I nodded.

I wanted to stay exactly like this for the rest of my vacation. Unfortunately, nature called.

When I returned from the bathroom, Drake was opening the curtain allowing daylight to filter into the room.

"What time is it?" I asked.

"Nine."

"Too early." I hopped back into the still-warm bed, sat with my knees up to my chest, and pulled the covers up to my neck.

Drake walked naked across the room, plumped the pillows against the headboard, and joined me.

I filled him in on my California inquiries.

"I flew into the Hanakapiai Valley again yesterday," he told me. "It was high tide, and I noticed that the spot where our dead guy ended up was quite a bit closer to the water's edge."

"Meaning?"

"Meaning that, if the tide was high the time of night he was killed, someone could have brought him around there by boat."

"How can we find out?"

"I already have. I checked the tide calendar. High tide last Friday night was eleven forty-two. And, there was an almost-full moon."

I pondered that. It still didn't seem very likely.

Page had been a good hundred yards from the water's edge. Even at high tide, someone would have had to lug his body sixty yards or more, up sloping terrain strewn with boulders. He hadn't been a large man by any means, but even at one-sixty, one-seventy, he would have been a burden to carry that far.

Besides, if they had a boat, why didn't they just dump him into the sea? Why go to all that extra trouble?

Unless they *wanted* it to look like a helicopter was involved.

I became distracted by Drake, who was planting a line of kisses across my ribcage, heading for my belly.

"I'm hungry," he murmured. "It's either macadamia nut pancakes or this."

It was a tough decision — I wanted both. I ran my fingers through his hair.

An hour later, we strolled though the lobby hand in hand.

"Let me stop at the desk, and see if there are any messages," I told Drake.

There was one, from Officer Akito. He wanted to see me today. Now that was a switch. I supposed I should comply, but first I wanted to talk to Mack again.

"Is Mack flying today?" I asked Drake, as we walked the perimeter of the hotel's curving driveway, heading for the parking lot.

He glanced at his watch. "Yeah, but he should have a lunch break about twelve. It's ten-thirty now. Let's get some breakfast, then catch him at the office."

My rental car hadn't been driven in two days, and I noticed a film of dried rain spots on it. There was also something white flapping under the left wiper blade. I grabbed at it without much interest, thinking it was probably a handbill of some kind. I slid into the driver's seat, and reached across to unlock Drake's door. I pressed the switch to lower the top, and stuck the key into the ignition before giving the white paper another glance.

Only then did I notice that it was an envelope, plain generic white, with cut-out magazine letters spelling CHARLIE pasted across the front. A funny prickling sensation formed at the base of my neck, and waves of goose bumps ran up both arms. My lungs seemed unable to expel the air in them, while my heart pounded in slow heavy thuds.

"Charlie?" Drake stared at me, two ridges of concern pulling his brows together.

I held the front of the envelope up for him to see. He got very still, waiting for me to open it.

I noticed that the envelope was fresh and unwrinkled with no sign of water spotting, like on the car. It must have been placed on the windshield this morning.

The flap ripped as my trembling fingers worked at it. Inside was a single sheet of paper, with more cut-out words and letters. GARVEY DID IT. BUTT OUT AND LET HIM FRY. I handed it over to Drake, while I grabbed a deep breath and started the car.

My mind raced through my list of suspects. No one seemed to particularly have it in for Mack, except Akito. Surely, the police wouldn't resort to this kind of tactic, even if the officer had a personal grievance with the suspect.

Among the others, I wasn't sure who would even know that Mack was the prime suspect at this point.

I drove mechanically, following the remembered back streets to the Tip Top Cafe. Neither of us spoke as I parked the car and we made our way to the same back-corner booth we'd taken before.

Drake and I were both quiet as we ordered pancakes and watched the waitress walk away. I felt unsettled.

Maybe it was just the effect of coming abruptly off a sexual high. Maybe it was the whole case, in general. I was antsy to talk to Mack again. There were things he hadn't told me, and now I wondered how much more I didn't know. I hated doubting him.

Our waitress ambled over, two plates of pancakes in hand. Her flame-red hair was ratted up high in front, one-dimensional, like a fake-fronted building on a movie set. There were precise little spikes of bangs arranged across her forehead. The rest of it formed a shoulder-length fluffy cloud. I found myself scanning my plate for hairs. I hoped the cook's coif was a bit more restrained than this one.

Drake and I both accepted more coffee before she left. I watched him drench his pancakes in syrup.

"What do you think?" I asked.

"You mean, who might have left the note?"

I nodded, cutting a wedge from my cakes. They were the tiniest bit crisp on the surface, just the way I love them.

"Joe? He's got a hell of a nasty temper."

"I thought about that. I got a small sample of it myself the other day. But, if the police think Mack did it, doesn't that implicate Joe, too? I'd think Joe would want to steer me in a different direction."

"Unless they come up with someone else who might have helped him."

"True. Who might that be?" I asked.

"They questioned *me* yesterday." He sopped up syrup with a slice of pancake. "I told them it would have been rather stupid of me to dump a body, then fly to the spot the very next day and lead them to it."

I didn't point out to him that the person who discovers the body frequently becomes the murder suspect. I had been with him when he first saw that body. There would have been no faking the reaction I'd seen.

We finished our coffee and drove to Mack's offices. Melanie fawned over Drake when she saw him, and I had to suppress the wave of . . . what? . . . jealousy? . . . that I felt. After all, she had known him longer than I had, and she'd still be here after I was gone. What *were* these feelings?

Drake brushed past her, asking if Mack was in. She plopped back into her chair with a small pout.

"Cute kid," he said, once we were partway down the hall, "but her circuits aren't quite all connected." He tapped at the side of his head.

For some odd reason, I felt better.

Mack sat at his desk, writing figures on a yellow pad with his right hand, clutching a sandwich in his left. I took the chair across from his desk. His khaki slacks had deep wrinkles in them and the navy knit shirt had come untucked on one side, making the company logo hang lopsided. The military straightness had gone out of his shoulders. The lines around his eyes looked deeper than before, the gray in his hair more obvious.

I hated to press him, but I had to.

"Mack, why didn't you tell me about the fight you and Gil had at the hangar Friday night?"

The color left his lips, and he swallowed hard. The sandwich hung loosely in his fingers, looking like it might fall. I sat very still, looking him straight in the eye, waiting.

"I . . . I didn't think anyone knew about that," he said finally.

"Joe overheard it. He's told the police the two of you sounded like you were going to tear each other apart."

"Now wait a minute! It wasn't anything like that." The life had come back into him, anyway. He planted the sandwich on a napkin on his desk and stood abruptly.

"Page called me at the office about nine o'clock. He wanted to meet me at the hangar. I suggested that he just come to the office, but he insisted on the hangar. I think he wanted the psychological advantage of making me look at my helicopter while telling me I was about to lose it."

He tucked the straggling shirt tail into the top of his pants as he paced toward the window. The short burst of energy lasted only until he got back to his chair. He slumped into it once again.

"Anyway, I met Gil there," he sighed. "He told me I had until the end of the week to come up with some other financing. He wanted the money back to give to his boy for a race car. I told him there was no way I could do it. Banks here just don't move that fast. I'd be lucky to get approval in a month, much less a week.

"I pointed out that taking the helicopter away from me wouldn't do either of us much good. He'd have to sell it to get his money, and the bottom has really fallen out of the used helicopter market the past few months. He probably wouldn't have been able to get back all his investment. And, then what would I do? I need that ship to keep the cash flowing."

He picked at the sandwich again, and turned to me, pleading his case. "We may have raised our voices a time or two, but it never got close to blows. He tried to bully me into coming up with a lump sum by the end of the week, but I just couldn't. I told him that."

"So that's how you left it?"

"Pretty much. He said he had one other possibility — some other place he might be able to get the money for his kid."

"Who left the hangar first, you or Gil?"

"I did," he said. "But I thought he was leaving right behind me. There were only my car and his in the lot. Hell, Joe's truck wasn't even there. How could he have heard this so-called fight?"

"He says he overheard your voices and didn't want to get involved, so he drove around for awhile."

"Joe's making a lot more of this than it really was, Charlie."

I wondered why. Clearly, one of them was lying to me. I looked over at Drake. He didn't say a word.

"I gotta go," Mack said. "I've got a flight in fifteen minutes." He jammed the last bite of sandwich into his mouth, while picking up his sunglasses and headset. Drake rose and clapped a hand on Mack's shoulder.

I lingered a moment as the two men started down the hall. Next to Mack's yellow pad lay a computer printout. My natural snoopiness would not let me walk past it without taking a peek.

Mack's quarterly financial statements didn't look so hot.

It only took a second for my eyes to skim down to the bottom line. The operation showed a loss for two of the three months. Flipping to the second page, his balance sheet was in no better shape. His long term liabilities nearly rivaled the national debt.

I turned back to the income statement and did a bit of fast math in my head. Given his gross sales and assuming they continued to fly a full schedule, Mack was barely making it. He'd simply gotten himself too far in debt. I wondered how long he'd had these figures.

Just how desperate was Mack Garvey?

I was about to walk away when something else caught my eye. Mack's legal expenses for the quarter were well over ten thousand dollars. Based on his overall picture, that seemed way out of line. What could he be involved in? The income statement didn't give a breakdown.

I glanced around the room, well aware that I really didn't belong here, but curious as hell about what I'd just seen. I dimly registered the closing of the front door and assumed Mack had left. Passengers for the upcoming flight were beginning to gather in the front waiting room. I could hear Drake's voice chatting with them. Melanie would surely be occupied with checking the people in.

I decided to risk a few more minutes.

Mack's desk drawers were unlocked, so I made myself at home in his chair, and pulled open the lower drawer on my right. Manila file folders were jammed in, along with a plastic box of staples, some loose envelopes, and a metal ruler whose rusty corners looked pretty deadly. However, it was the files that interested me. I flipped through them quickly.

The fourth one back was labeled LEGAL. People make this so easy.

The file was thick, and there was no time to study it carefully, but I was able to get the gist pretty quickly. Mack was being sued. By Bill Steiner. The pilot I'd seen at the heliport that first day. The man who'd made such a scene with one of his own employees.

According to the petition, Steiner was suing to gain control of Mack's landing pad at the heliport. Some of the correspondence in the file had gotten pretty heated. There were a number of letters back and forth between Mack and his attorney. Mack's letters had a sense of desperation. No wonder. Without a landing pad, he wouldn't be in business another day. The bills would keep coming, but the money wouldn't.

The question was, could this possibly be connected to the Gil Page situation?

10

Drake and I decided it was time to stop by the police station. I wasn't eager for another meeting with Akito, but I was curious why he had left a message for me. And, I thought he should know about my trip to California. I hadn't yet decided whether I would tell him about the note on my car. It might serve to sway him further against Mack. I needed to know more myself before I let Akito in on that little tidbit.

Susan Turner was leaning against the duty sergeant's desk when we walked in. She wore a white halter-top sundress. The back was completely bare, and there were enough cutouts along her ribcage that the little remaining fabric was merely a formality. The skirt consisted of two rows of ruffles, and hit her about six inches above the knee.

Her long blond hair was loose this time, brushing the middle of her bare back in soft curls. She had a large red hibiscus tucked behind her right ear. A red bangle bracelet decorated her left arm, and red pumps with four inch heels completed the ensemble.

"I don't see why I can't go back to California now," she pressed. "I've got a business to run. Things just don't go right without the boss there."

The duty officer sat back, implacable. His dusky face, smooth as coffee laced with cream, didn't budge.

"Akito's orders," was all he said. His eyes dropped to her cleavage.

Susan turned slightly just then, and caught sight of me. A funny look came over her face, like a kid who's been caught earnestly telling a whopping lie. She didn't know I'd visited California, but somehow she knew that I knew she was full of shit.

I didn't say a word.

Susan flashed one final look of irritation toward the officer at the desk, then turned abruptly. Her short skirt flounced upward, giving the men one nice leg shot. A cloud of Emeraude descended chokingly when she passed. It took a full minute for the air to become breatheable after she walked out.

Officer Akito wasn't in, and wouldn't be the rest of the day, I was informed. I told the sergeant on duty briefly why I had come, and he took a few notes. I wasn't convinced he really gave a damn, one way or the other, but at least I had done my civic duty.

Drake took my hand as we walked down the steps.

"You need a break," he said. "How about coming out to my place?"

"To see your etchings?" I teased.

"Well, I'm fresh out of etchings right now, but I can cook a pretty decent steak."

"Sounds good to me." I leaned over for another quick sample of his mouth.

We drove back to the hotel to pick up his truck and leave the rental. It was nice to be chauffeured. As a driver, I'd been so intent on the traffic I hadn't had a chance to do much sightseeing here.

The ocean reflected the deep blue sky, and I enjoyed the glimpses of shoreline I got now and then as we traveled highway 56 toward Kapaa, the island's largest town. Fields of sugar cane surrounded us, like disorderly corn stalks, fallen out of their ranks and hanging around in clumps.

As we neared the Wailua River, I could see a long stretch of coastline — palm trees in the foreground, the brilliant blue water laced with white foam, the distant mountains hazy in the humid air. A few people stretched out on towels or lounge chairs on the sand, while half a dozen local boys on boogie boards braved the churning surf.

Just beyond the river, we turned inland. Groves of coconut palms flanked the road on the right, while the other side boasted flowering plumeria trees in showy clusters of brilliant white, yellow and pink. The road began to climb and the area became residential. A couple of turns brought us again into open fields with few houses. Drake guided the truck into a narrow lane.

He called his house a cottage. He had built it himself right after his divorce. He shyly told me I was the first woman he'd brought here.

It was a tiny place, cozy and remarkably homey for a bachelor's house. It sat on a large lot, an acre or so, and was nestled among mango, banana, and papaya trees. A Norfolk pine at the back of the house must have stood at least sixty feet tall. Beyond the trees, I glimpsed the top of the immense Waialeale crater. Today, again, the crest was obscured by a topping of wispy cloud.

The cottage was rectangular, one short end being the front. That entire side was taken up with windows facing out over the valley. The Hawaiian style roof rose steeply to a high peak. The exterior was painted pale gray with white trim. A deck railing of white circled the perimeter.

Inside, everything was neat and compact. There was a good-sized living room which took full advantage of the view from the large picture windows. The small kitchen featured built-in appliances, including a stacked washer/dryer. A pineapple, left to ripen on the counter, filled the air with sweet perfume.

The bedroom and bath were small, too, but neatly arranged with places built in for everything. The bed was covered with a blue and white quilt, obviously hand-made.

Helicopter memorabilia decorated the walls, and Drake spent some time taking me around to view each item. He had artifacts from a couple of stints in South America, a deadly-looking spear gun from some remote south Pacific island, and pictures of himself flying various aircraft in locations ranging from the ice-white wilderness of Alaska to the scene of a fourteen car pileup on a lonely stretch of Nevada highway.

"This is the most tame my life has ever been," he told me. "Going to work each morning, and coming home every night is a real luxury in this profession."

I sensed a hint of regret in his voice and wondered if that had been the problem in his marriage. It must be hard to keep a relationship going when you can't be together much. And yet, they had stuck it out a long time. I had to admire that — me, whose only long-term relationship has been living with my dog for ten years.

He poured two glasses of white wine, and we took them out to the deck which circled the house on three sides. The Wailua Valley stretched out before us. Acres of ranch land lay all around. Cattle, horses, and goats grazed in neatly fenced pastures. I couldn't remember ever seeing this much green in my life. Like most tourists, I'd had no idea that Hawaii didn't consist entirely of lava cliffs, sandy beaches, and palm trees.

The sky was clear and a light warm breeze swept over us. I thought of the chill April winds we'd had at home for the past month. This felt like heaven.

The wine coursed through my body, and I began to feel completely relaxed for the first time in days. No matter how much I'd tried to convince myself that I was on vacation, and Mack's problems were not mine, anytime I'm on a case, I begin to take it personally. It's just me.

Drake reached out and stroked my cheek with the back of his index finger.

"You needed an afternoon off," he said.

The sun was setting behind the extinct crater as we cooked a couple of steaks on the hibachi. I watched in silence as he expertly blended ingredients for a Caesar salad.

"Just because a guy lives alone doesn't mean he has to subsist on fast food," he said, catching my fascinated stare.

I didn't want to admit to him that I'm basically a microwave person myself. It's just so much easier when cooking for one.

He spread a cloth out on his small table and lit a candle for the middle. A romantic man of many talents. I had never met anyone quite like him.

After dinner, he put on soft music and we talked a lot, stopping to dance together in the living room whenever a good song came on. When he offered the use of a spare toothbrush if I'd stay the night, I accepted.

11

I awakened to a gentle nudging.

"Come on." Drake reached his arm around my waist and murmured into my neck. "This is my last morning off this week, and we're going to use it to good advantage."

After last night, I marvelled at the man's stamina but it turned out he had something else in mind. By the time I'd finished a revitalizing five minutes under the hot shower and slipped back into my jeans and t-shirt, I could hear him rummaging around outside. I went to investigate. He was digging through a crowded storage room at the back of the house.

"I've got an extra helmet in here somewhere," he muttered, poking his head up over a dusty cardboard box. A quick movement on the door jamb caught my attention and I jumped back, drawing in a sharp breath that was just short of a shriek.

"Only a gecko," Drake assured me.

The small brown lizard-thing slithered up the side of the house, away from me. I took a couple of quick breaths and faked a smile, not wanting to be too much of a sissy. Drake was back up to his elbows in a cardboard box, paying no attention to the pounding sound my heart was making.

I didn't offer to help him. I knew the small, crowded, dusty place probably harbored a wealth of bugs, lizards, and other creepy unmentionables. It took a couple of minutes for my pulse to settle down.

In the meantime, Drake emerged with two helmets in hand.

I looked past the storeroom, and saw a gleaming black Honda motorcycle parked beside the house. It was one of those big touring bikes built for two. Would the many facets of this man never cease to amaze me?

"I even dusted off the cobwebs for you," he said, extending the helmet.

I took the headgear from him, and surreptitiously peeked inside. All clear. I tucked my hair behind my ears and tried it on for size. Pretty close.

"You've been so busy spending your vacation helping my friend," he said, "that I want to treat you to a morning away from it all."

"I thought that's what last night was for," I told him.

"Umm, so it was. Well, you need to get a look at some of the island, too."

He started the bike and let it idle while he went back to lock the front door.

"Climb on," he invited, once he was seated. Each of the helmets was rigged with a small microphone so we could converse over the noise of the engine.

I'd forgotten how much fun it is to get out on the road like this. My motorcycle days had been confined to a few weeks back in high school when I dated a wild guy with a Harley. It had been right after my parents died, and I guess I did some pretty crazy things. Looking back, it's probably amazing I made it through that time alive.

Drake rode with the caution that naturally comes with middle age, although he fully enjoyed the power of the machine and its closeness to the road. His expert handling of the bike through traffic soon reassured me.

We headed north, toward Hanalei. High clouds dotted the sky in puffs, none threatening. Today, the ocean was a deep gray-blue, the surf higher than I'd seen before. The same local boys on their boogie boards dotted the water around Wailua, but apparently it was too rough for the tourists to handle. All the vehicles along the small beach were local trucks or rusted out island cars — no rentals.

Traffic became a heavy slow-moving stream as we approached Kapaa. There was no alternative but to get in line and adjust to the leisurely pace.

We passed little strip shopping centers filled with small touristy clothing shops. I wondered how many of them could survive. There was a McDonald's on our left, then a Safeway — little familiarities in an atmosphere that was otherwise exotic to me.

Occasionally, a driver in the endless line would pause, waving through some poor soul who wanted to join in from a side street. This driver courtesy was one more foreign idea to me. I commented on it to Drake.

"Hey, this *is* life in the fast lane here," he replied.

There was a certain appeal to the unhurried pace, the idea that life could exist without blaring horns and the one-finger salute from other drivers. Whether I could really ever settle into it, I wasn't sure.

We passed most of the commercial buildings and, within a few minutes, left the thickest of the populated area behind.

On the open road, I breathed deeply of the fishy sea air. Soon, the road curved inland enough that we only had occasional glimpses of the water. We cruised past small housing developments with tiny yards where people had set up stands to sell flower leis, and the bananas, papayas, and coconuts which grew beside the houses. When we weren't talking on the intercom, FM radio played.

Along the way, Drake pointed out historic sites dating back to the mid-eighteen hundreds when the missionaries came. At Princeville, a modern resort community, he stopped at a small market. We bought sandwiches and sodas for a picnic lunch. He tucked the bag inside his light jacket and we headed north once more.

The highway became narrow as it wound down into the Hanalei Valley. A brilliant green patchwork of taro fields covered the valley floor, and we crossed several one-lane bridges before passing through Hanalei.

"Lumahai Beach is one of our better known," Drake told me, "the one where the movie *South Pacific* was filmed."

I remembered it from the helicopter tour. Drake guided the Honda off to the side and parked under the trees to have our sandwiches. The water was turquoise in the protected bay, darkening beyond the reef to a rich, deep blue. The sand was choppy with footprints, although we saw no one.

"I feel guilty, taking time off for sightseeing when Mack is still under suspicion," I told Drake.

He lifted the tab on his soda can. It fizzed briefly, releasing pressure. "Look, you're on vacation here. You are already doing Mack a huge favor, putting in this much time on the case. You can afford one morning to relax."

"I know, but I tend to get restless when something's unsolved. I feel like I need to be working."

"What do you have so far? Who are your suspects?"

"I guess Catherine Page tops my list. She admitted to me the other day that she hated Gil with a passion. I've seen women like her before, Drake. They live with an abusive man for years, letting themselves get pushed around and pushed around. Then, something gives. They just can't take it anymore. Usually, they'll just divorce the guy, leaving him wondering what went wrong. Because the woman hasn't been allowed to voice a complaint for years, and because the men are absolutely blind to their own behavior, the husband usually has no idea why she left."

"So, why wouldn't Catherine have simply left Gil?"

"Hard to say, but I'd guess the reason had to do with her son, and money. She might not have been forceful enough to push for her rights under California's community property laws, and she might have felt that she'd never get a fair shake. It's a pretty sure bet that Gil could and would have hired the toughest attorney he could find.

"Also, I got the distinct impression that she and Joe Esposito know each other. Catherine wouldn't have had the nerve to deliver the fatal blow personally, but she could have paid someone to do it. Someone with a hot temper."

"But, Joe?"

"How well do you know him, Drake? Maybe I'm wrong."

"I guess I really don't know him that well," he admitted. "When I started working for Mack three years ago, Joe was already his mechanic. He keeps pretty much to himself. Most of the Portuguese here do. They hang around together, but don't mix much with others. I think he likes the cock fights on Saturday nights — I've heard him mention that a couple of times. Heck, I don't even know whether he has a family."

"Well, I don't know. I'm still looking for some evidence. At this point, all I have are suspicions."

A flicker of a thought crossed my mind — something Mack had said yesterday.

"Drake, remember when Mack said he left the hangar after the argument with Page?"

"Yeah."

"He said Joe's truck wasn't in the parking lot. He said his car and Gil's were the only two out there. If Gil was killed at the hangar, then what happened to his car?"

My mind tried to reconstruct the rest of the conversation, to find some kind of thread I could grasp.

"Mack looked pretty distraught yesterday," Drake said. "Maybe he's got things mixed up. I like Mack, and I sure want to think he's innocent."

"But, you have some doubt?"

He carefully folded the plastic wrap from his sandwich into a tiny square and stared at it, squeezing it between his fingers before answering.

"Drake?"

"Remember the morning I took the first flight for Mack? The morning after he'd been arrested?"

I nodded, and waited to see what he was getting at.

"When I entered my flight time in the aircraft logbook, I rechecked the math back over the previous week. It's force of habit with me since the maintenance schedule is based on the number of hours flown. I've always made it a habit to recheck the hours every week or two."

Something about this was making him uncomfortable, but I let him take his time.

"Anyway, the figures Mack had written in for Friday looked to me like they might have been changed. A number that had been written in as a three, had been changed to a two." He paused, and I watched him wrestle with the problem.

"What does that mean, Drake?"

"Well it could be innocent, Charlie. I mean, we've all done it, where we write something down wrong, and then scratch in the correct figure over it."

"But, this just *happened* to be Friday night, right?"

"Right."

"And, what would it mean if the two was really supposed to be a three?"

"It would mean that the aircraft was flown an hour longer than the record shows it was. An hour would have easily been enough time to fly to the Hanakapiai and back."

12

I felt badly for Drake, having to voice suspicions against his friend. I thought of the financial statements I'd seen on Mack's desk the day before. It worried me, too, that I might eventually have to present evidence against Mack. That kind of situation had never happened to me before, and I wasn't sure how I'd handle it.

The matter of the argument at the maintenance hangar bothered me still. Mack had lied by omission when he hadn't told me about it until I questioned him. Then, when he did finally admit it, his version and Joe's were so different.

Who was lying, and why?

I stared out at the water, and rubbed my aching temples.

I was supposed to be on Mack's side. I hated doubting him.

Drake moved around behind me and began to massage my shoulders. It felt good, a reassurance that someone had confidence in me.

"Come on," he said, patting my behind. "Let's ride the rest of the way to the end of the road."

We remounted the motorcycle and he plugged my headphone into the intercom system once again. We passed a few scattered businesses along the road, mostly unimposing little real estate offices and boogie board rental shops, but one caught my eye. Boat rentals. Their sign announced that they had daily and weekly rates.

"Drake?" I interrupted an instrumental rendition of "Can't Buy Me Love."

"How far are we from the Hanakapiai Valley?"

"When we get to the end of the road, it's not far at all. I can show you."

Ten or fifteen minutes later, we were there. The end of the road spread out to form a small parking lot. Perhaps two dozen cars, all rentals, were parked on both sides of the last stretch of pavement. There weren't many people in evidence, though.

We cruised slowly through the lot.

One young couple, wearing neon pink baseball caps, stood at the trunk of their car. They were apparently having a heated discussion over who would be in charge of the camera.

After a short bout of verbal back-and-forth, the girl grabbed the camera and slammed the trunk closed. We watched him follow timidly as she stomped toward the woods.

Their matching shirts said "Just Maui'd."

A gray-haired sixty-ish couple emerged near the spot where the young couple had just disappeared. They walked slowly back toward their car from the direction of the beach. He went about elaborate detours to avoid getting his sparkling white canvas shoes near mud puddles, while she chose the direct route, arriving at the car well ahead of him.

"Where are all the other people?" I asked Drake, looking around at the number of unoccupied cars in the lot.

"Probably hiking the trail," he replied. "This is the head of the only trail that leads up the Na Pali coast. Remember, I pointed it out on the tour?"

Now that he mentioned it, I did. It looked different from this end, though.

He pulled the bike into a relatively protected spot. The clouds overhead had begun to look threatening so he chose a place under the trees. We dismounted and he showed me the way.

The well-worn path was strewn with leaves, brown and soggy now, trampled into a sort of mushy carpet. Three beer cans and a plastic grocery sack had been tossed to the side. The remains of a campfire on the beach lay scattered over a wide area.

Once we stepped out into the open, the view up the coast was incredible. The wind blew fresh off the sea, the air laden with moisture. There ahead of us, enshrouded in mist, stood row after row of razor-like peaks, like the stand-up plates on the back of a Stegosaurus. They appeared lavender gray in the afternoon mist. I felt a little breathless.

"They look so much bigger from ground level," I told Drake. "Even for a kid raised in the Rockies, I have to say, this is spectacular."

"Hanakapiai Valley is the first one," he said, pointing. "Right between those two ridges."

I turned to look all around me. If a person rented one of those Zodiac boats with a motor, they could easily pull it up out of the water around here somewhere. Then, they might drive back later, maybe with a body in the trunk, retrieve the boat, and buzz over to that valley.

This knowledge didn't exactly help me zero in on a suspect. Any of them could have managed it quite easily.

I decided a visit to the boat rental places would be in order.

I asked Drake if he would mind stopping on the way back. The shop I remembered seeing might be a good possibility. In order for the killer to have used the boat overnight, they'd just about have to rent it for longer than a day. Otherwise, the rental shop would expect it back the same afternoon it was taken out.

The breeze off the ocean had turned chill, the clouds dark overhead. We walked a short way up the trail but soon turned back, coated with goose bumps. Drake slipped his arm around my shoulders, chafing at my upper arm to warm it. We dashed for the Honda just as the first few raindrops spattered us.

A half-mile down the road, we were soaked. Frigid wind and water pasted my t-shirt to my skin. I clung even closer to Drake's hunched back.

Abruptly, the rain ended and within minutes we had slipped out from under the clouds and into the sunshine. By the time we neared the boat rental shop the wind had whipped our shirts dry. I didn't want to think about how I looked; at least my nipples weren't standing straight out anymore.

Drake slowed to watch for the place.

Their sign was the color of a taxi cab, with letters of process blue. Easy to spot. The business was situated in a little wooden shack, which had presumably been a plantation cottage in the old days. We pulled up beside it, parking the bike on the grass. I could practically hear the termites chewing away at the short wood pilings on which the small building stood.

A layer of dried red mud coated its steps, porch and floor. Bright neon boogie boards leaned against the walls outside. The door stood open so we walked in.

A wooden counter divided the tiny room in half. Our side of the room had additional boards stacked against the exterior walls but nothing else in the way of furnishings. The counter top held two brochure racks which carried a variety of folders describing the activities one could partake of here. Helicopter tours, fishing charters, and luaus seemed to top the list.

A young man stood behind the counter, ruffling through a bunch of notices tacked to a bulletin board behind him. The notices looked like the neighborhood answer to a penny shopper newspaper. The ones I could read at a distance appeared to list various items for sale, including one "not very rusty" refrigerator.

The guy had shoulder length blond hair, bleached by the sun, and looking like he'd come out of the sea without bothering to comb through it. He wore a pair of baggy shorts that rode so low on his skinny hips, I found it embarrassing. No shirt. He flipped long strands of bangs out of his face as he turned to face us. I caught a whiff of pot.

"Howzit?" he greeted. I guessed it was the island version of "May I help you?"

"Yeah," I said, "I'd like some information about the boats you rent. You have some with motors?"

Given the distance involved and the strength of the waves I'd seen, I couldn't imagine any one managing it with a paddle.

"Sure do," he answered proudly. "The only place on the north shore that has 'em. All the others are kayaks and boogie boards."

Good. This was going to cut my search time by quite a bit.

"I need to know if someone rented one within the last week, and kept it overnight."

"Nope."

"Are you sure? I mean, maybe you should check your rental receipts, or something."

"I know we didn't."

His sureness irritated me.

I pulled out my card. "It pertains to a murder investigation. I would appreciate it if you would double check."

He pulled out a cardboard box with frayed edges, about four by six inches big, two inches deep. He drew out all the receipts that were in it, a stack about a half inch thick.

"Kayak, kayak, boogie board. . ." He read off the rental item from each one, as he pointedly slapped it down on the counter.

There was only one Zodiac rental for the week, and it had been returned by five o'clock on the same day it was rented. I hated the smug look he flashed at me when he was through.

"And there are no others still out?"

This time, when he said no, I didn't push it.

Once we were on the road again, I asked Drake: "Where else could a person get their hands on one of those boats?"

"You might check the yellow pages when we get back," he said. "Business is so competitive here, these guys will all tell you they're the only one that provides a service. I have to say, though, I don't know of any others myself."

He had paperwork to do that afternoon so he took me back to the hotel. We made plans to see each other again that night.

I went to my room to make phone calls but didn't get much in the way of results.

Several companies were listed who gave boat tours along the coast using Zodiac boats, but none of them rented their boats out to individuals. Our stringy-haired friend was apparently correct again when he told me that they were the only one who provided motorized rentals.

After a half-dozen calls, I gave up, frustrated that my theory hadn't worked out.

I sat at the table, staring at the silent phone and tapping my nails on the wooden surface. I needed to ask one more favor of Morton, my friendly concierge. I hoped I could get this one for less than twenty bucks.

I picked up the receiver once again and dialed his extension.

"Hi, Morton. Charlie Parker." My voice sounded saccharin, even to me. I hate sucking up although it *is* an efficient means of getting information.

"Hello, Ms. Parker." His tone was equally sickening.

"I need one teensy favor, if you could."

"Certainly," he gushed, "whatever I can do."

"Mr. Page, who was registered in ten-fifty-nine, received a call last Friday night. Would your computers show what number the call came from?"

"An incoming call? Afraid not. We only have records of outgoing numbers."

Rats. I was afraid of this.

"Oh, one other thing," I persisted. "What time of day did Mrs. Page check in?"

I waited on hold while he went to a terminal and signed on. He was back a moment later.

"Ten a.m. on Sunday."

Wow. She must have been at the airport within minutes after receiving the news of her widowhood. I wondered if there was a way to find out when her ticket had been booked. There was the possibility that she'd flown to the island a day earlier, say, right after the telephone argument.

Or, what if the phone argument had been staged?

Maybe the call didn't come from California at all.

All this ran through my mind as I thanked Morton, and hung up. I calculated the time on the west coast. Late afternoon already. I wondered if I'd reach anyone in the phone company's business office. It was worth a shot.

After dialing Information for the number, I got a perky sounding girl named Pamela on the line.

"Yes, Pamela, this is Catherine Page. Mrs. Gilbert Page." I gave the Page's home phone number. "I need to find out whether a call was placed from my home last Friday night to this number in Hawaii." I gave her the number at the Westin.

"I'm sorry, Mrs. Page," she said, "I only have access to billing records during normal business hours, eight to five, Monday through Friday."

"Oh, dear," I said, sounding as put-out as I could.

"Wouldn't it just be simpler to wait until your bill comes? If you are charged incorrectly for a call, we'll be happy to credit you."

"Oh, it's not that. Actually, I hope there was a call and I need to know today. See, my son is home alone. My husband and I are on vacation in Hawaii. Jason says he was home, and in fact called us from there, but I suspect he's been staying with that girlfriend of his. She's a little tart, you know."

I could practically hear Pamela's eyes roll back. God, what a bitch, she was thinking.

"I'm sorry, ma'am. Tomorrow morning would be the soonest I could find out. I could call you then."

Great. That's all I needed. She'd ask for Catherine Page's room and feed her the information. How do I get myself into these things?

"Let me call you back," I suggested. "We're checking out early."

She seemed glad to get rid of me.

Next, I put in a call to Catherine Page. I was curious whether the police had also asked her to stick around for awhile. The desk told me she had not checked out, but she wasn't in her room, either.

There was still no one among the people I'd interviewed who had seen Gil Page alive after the alleged argument with Mack. I needed to find such a witness, if there was one. I also thought it would be nice to find someone else who could verify either Mack's or Joe's version of that exchange. Maybe another trip out to the airport was in order.

I retrieved the rental from the hotel lot, started it and allowed it to idle for a couple of minutes, since it hadn't been driven in more than a day. Traffic was light — I arrived at the airport in less than ten minutes.

The maintenance area was beginning to feel like a second home to me. I whipped into the parking lot like a regular, taking the third space from the end.

The little three-sided wooden structure was occupied, this time by a man. He was seventy if he was a day, standing approximately five foot two, weighing in at close to a hundred pounds. One sure bet, if the Iraqis decided this was the airport they wanted to invade, this guy would not pose a formidable threat.

He rose from the four-legged metal stool the state had provided for his comfort and held his ground, awaiting my approach. I didn't make any sudden moves. Although it probably would have taken him a good four or five minutes to wrestle his gun from its holster, once he did, that trigger finger didn't look any too steady.

"Hi," I said tentatively.

"Where's your badge?" His sharp black eyes scanned me, as he growled the words.

"I don't want in," I assured him. "I just need to ask a question."

He continued to regard me with suspicion until I reached the fence. A jet took off on the nearest runway just then, so I waited until the noise had subsided.

"Were you on duty here last Friday night, about ten o'clock?" I asked.

"Friday night." He rubbed his gums together for a couple of very long minutes. "Nope."

He turned away from me, heading back to his comfy seat. I guess he took me literally when I said I wanted to ask *a* question.

"Wait. Do you know who was on duty that night?"

"Nope."

This guy was just a wealth of information, I must say.

"Can you tell me where I can find out?" I hate to be pushy, especially with our senior citizens, but really.

"Head of security. Over't the security office." He waved vaguely in the direction of the airport terminal building.

I smiled as large a smile as I could muster and thanked him. I don't know whether he noticed or not. He seemed intent on getting off his feet as soon as he could.

I had no idea where I was going, but it seemed like the main terminal building would be a good starting place. Leaving the parking lot by the maintenance hangars, I had to drive past the helipads. Mack's helicopter was gone. Instinctively, I glanced at my watch. It was almost three. Drake had told me their last flight was usually at four.

Without too much difficulty, I managed to follow the loop that led me to the main airport parking area. A flimsy yellow automatic arm stopped me from entering the lot. I pulled a ticket from the machine and the arm obligingly raised to admit me.

I parked three rows in and found my way to the crosswalk which was supposed to get me safely across four lanes of traffic. Luck was with me and I spotted a traffic officer who was wearing the same HPA uniform as the gate guards.

He was considerably more on the ball than his senior counterpart at the maintenance area. He directed me to the security office.

Inside, a pear-shaped female officer sat behind a scuffed metal desk. The back legs of her metal chair were firmly planted on the linoleum floor, the chair back resting against the wall. I could see a long metal-colored mark on the paint indicating that this was a common position here. My sixth grade teacher, Mrs. Singer, would have rapped her knuckles with a ruler for that.

Her blue and gray uniform might have fit correctly once, about three children ago. Now it was stretched across her bulging mid-section in imminent danger of splitting at the seams. Her body tapered inward at the top, making her average sized breasts appear proportionately small.

Her long dark hair had been pulled back from her face, and twisted into an elaborate knot on top of her head. Two lacquered chopsticks skewered the knot in place somehow. I puzzled over this for a minute, wondering if it was painful. Three plumeria flowers stuck out from behind her right ear, perfuming the air in the small office.

I had caught her in the middle of a phone conversation, but she didn't let it bother her. I stood at the counter while she continued to commiserate with someone named Tessie whose husband, Keoki, slapped her around from time to time. Neither of them appeared to regard this as particularly critical. It was just something that Tessie didn't like very much.

I eavesdropped shamelessly while I checked out the surroundings.

The room was about fifteen feet wide by maybe twenty-five deep. A formica counter split the space and there were two metal desks behind it. The unoccupied one was piled high with folders and a scattering of loose memos. A short stack of unopened mail sat precisely in the center. The name plate facing me indicated Mr. Keala occupied this desk. Two gray file cabinets behind the desk had the locks pressed in.

Apparently, he was the busier of the two.

By contrast, the desk occupied by the woman was almost clear. A coffee cup with red waxy smears around the rim and a pack of Virginia Slims were the only evidence I could see of work in progress. Her stapler, tape dispenser, calculator, and phone were all neatly aligned around the edges of the desktop.

Posters on the walls behind her conspicuously detailed her rights under the Federal Wage and Hour Law and OSHA safety standards. On my side of the room, the posters were meant to inspire, with slogans such as "Security is Everybody's Business."

After ten minutes, I was tired of hearing Tessie's woes. I cleared my throat and glanced at my watch.

"Hold on a minute, Tess," the officer told her friend. She held the phone against her shoulder and raised her eyes to me.

"Can I help you?" she asked, in a tone that said my business better be urgent.

I was beginning to see why Drake said most people moving here from the mainland soon go nuts or go back. Some of these people had no concept that a fast lane even exists, much less what it might be like to live there. Trying to accomplish even the simplest tasks felt like living in one of those slow moving dreams where you're walking through an atmosphere as thick as gel.

"I need to know some information about the guard's work schedule," I told her. "Specifically, which guard was working the gate near the helicopter maintenance hangars last Friday night around ten p.m."

"Who's asking?" She narrowed her eyes suspiciously.

I opened my wallet, flashing my driver's license toward her. If she wanted to question it, she was going to have to move her fat ass out of the chair.

"Tess, I'll call you back," she said to the phone.

Tipping her chair down in slow motion, she rose to approach the counter. Her name tag told me she was Beatrice.

"Now, what exactly is it you want?" she asked.

I thought I had been fairly specific, but I repeated the request.

"I don't know," she said. "I probably better check with a supervisor before I give out that kind of information. That's Mr. Keala. He won't be back until Monday."

Four more days. No way I was going to let this lady stall me that long. I gritted my teeth to keep my impatience from showing.

"Beatrice," I smiled, trying a different tactic, "I really started out all wrong with you, didn't I? First off, I should apologize for interrupting your phone conversation."

She was still wary, unsure whether I was being serious or facetious.

"You and Tessie obviously have some important things to discuss. If I had the name I need, I could get out of your way, and you could resume your conversation."

She narrowed her eyes, probably wondering if I would turn her in to the supervisor.

"Actually," I continued, "maybe you and Tessie would rather keep your conversation private. Discuss this, say, over lunch? In fact, since I interrupted the conversation, maybe I could treat the two of you to lunch?"

I pulled a twenty out of my purse.

A black three-ring binder appeared from under the counter as if by magic. She flipped through a couple of sheets to locate the correct date. I wrote down the name her index finger pointed at. Willie Duran.

"When is Willie working next?"

She flipped forward one page. "Tomorrow. Same gate, seven to three."

"Have a nice lunch," I said, sliding the twenty across the counter.

Stepping out of the air conditioned office, the humidity hit me again like a blast. The four traffic lanes outside the terminal were jammed with cars. The combination of exhaust fumes and flowers made my throat want to close up.

The front of the terminal was completely open to the street so I stepped inside, hoping to get a little distance from the cars. I found pay phones near the Hawaiian Airlines ticket counter. One stall actually had a phone book intact.

There were two Willie (not William) Durans listed. Senior and Junior. I wrote them both down. I'd try Junior first. The address given was on Kuamoo Road (pronounced koo-ah-mo-oh according to my guidebook).

In Hawaiian, each vowel forms a separate syllable, and they are always pronounced one way. Unlike English, which must confuse the hell out of people trying to learn our crazy language.

The street maps in the front of the phone book showed Kuamoo to be between the towns of Lihue and Kapaa, maybe five miles or so from the airport.

I paid the parking attendant my fifty cents and headed back out Ahukini Road to Kuhio Highway. Past the golf course and just over the Wailua River, I saw the turn.

Now I recognized this as the same way I had come with Drake to his house. Kuamoo took me through part of an old coconut plantation and some low-lying fields flooded with water. I wondered whether they grew rice or taro there.

I'd have to ask Drake.

The road began to climb, taking me past a large waterfall. A parking lot beside the road was crowded with tourists who wandered to a lookout point and aimed their cameras toward the waterfall.

Beyond the fall, the area turned residential. I began to watch addresses. I passed the turnoff to Drake's place before the numbers started to get close to the one I was looking for. I slowed down, risking the wrath of a black pickup truck behind me, who was inches from my bumper.

Finally, I spotted the number I was looking for. There were two houses on the lot. A two-track dirt lane at the edge of the property took me to the back one.

The square wooden house had once been painted brown. Where the paint had chipped away, the wood beneath was weathered gray, giving the structure a mottled appearance, like a toad with a skin condition. Blotches of rust stained the corrugated metal roof as if some giant bird had flown by and done its thing.

A shiny new four-door blue Honda with a child seat in back sat near the front door. I parked beside it.

Ti plants grew in a scraggly line along the front of the house, providing the only attempt at landscaping. A banana palm near the front steps leaned precariously, laden with an almost ripe head of bananas.

The grass immediately around the house had been mowed, the effort ending abruptly about twenty feet out. A Ford van, apparently not operational, was parked against one side of the building. I noticed the mower had detoured around it, leaving grass over a foot tall growing around its tires.

A generic dog of possible beagle/pit bull ancestry trotted out to my car and lifted his leg on the back tire. His territory thus established, he seemed friendly enough. I got out and approached the house. The dog ignored me, finding his way to a shady spot under the banana tree.

It was then I noticed the young woman watching me. Standing behind the brownish screen door, I hadn't seen her. I wondered if she had watched me drive up. She held an infant balanced on her hip. The baby was trying to stuff fistfuls of the woman's hair into his mouth. She didn't seem to notice. I approached the door and caught the strong scent of diapers.

"Hi, I'm looking for Willie Duran," I said.

Her eyes narrowed, suspicious of my motives. "He's not here."

"Do you know when he might be back?"

She made no move to open the screen door. Beyond it, I could see that a toddler had a tight grip on her leg. I tried to see into the dim house without appearing to stare. The TV was turned up loud, Oprah announcing that her guests today would be victims of lesbian sexual assault. As intriguing as that sounded, I turned my attention back to my hostess.

"Are you Mrs. Duran?" I asked, attempting to get *something* out of her. She nodded. "I don't know when he be back. He go out for beer." In pidgin, it sounded like be-ah.

"Does he work at the airport?"

"Yeah, but he no work today. Tomorrow."

"Okay, I'll catch him later."

I jumped at the sound of a shriek behind me.

Two more children, boys no more than three or four years old, rounded the house and disappeared around the other side.

I looked back at the woman. She didn't look more than twenty or twenty-one. She had probably been a cute little thing in high school. Her face showed good bone structure and nice eyes, but her body had rounded out. She wore a faded purple T-shirt with a black Local Motion logo on it and stained white shorts. There was a large spot of grease or spit-up over her right breast. She had a hickey on her neck the size of a quarter.

What a life.

I decided not to leave my card. I didn't want Willie to have time to think about what he'd say to me. Not being familiar with the good ol' boy network here, I couldn't be sure he and Joe Esposito weren't golfing chums at the same country club.

I got back into my car and fitted the key into the ignition. As I backed out, the two little boys reappeared, each carrying two yellowish fruits about the size of tennis balls. They giggled and tried to hurl their ammunition at my car.

Fortunately, a three year old's range is only a couple of feet.

It was not quite four o'clock and the dark clouds we had seen earlier had moved inland, leaving this side of the island in bright sunshine. Maybe I'd just go back to the hotel and lay around the pool for an hour or so. I'd still have time to shower and dress for dinner that night with Drake. He had mentioned wanting to take me somewhere nice.

Thirty minutes later, I was again making the rounds of the lounge chairs surrounding the pool. I had brought my notebook along, thinking I would read back over my notes. Possibly, a new inspiration might hit me.

"Hi, Charlie!" The female voice came from my left as I circled the pool and I turned to see who it could be.

It was Susan Turner, looking tanned and fit, stretched out on her stomach. She patted the empty lounge chair next to her own. She was not exactly my idea of great company, but what the hell, maybe I could learn something new about Gil from her.

I felt decidedly flabby as I settled into the chair. Susan's lime-green bikini left absolutely nothing to the imagination. The top appeared to be nothing more than a band of stretchy cloth, pinched together in front between her breasts, which, from this angle, looked ready to spill over the top. The bottom of the suit was a G-string, leaving both buns fully exposed. She had the firmest looking glutes I'd ever seen. Her skin was the color of caramel, without a tan-line showing anywhere.

She swung her long legs around and sat up. At least I didn't have to talk to her rear end.

I noticed that her every move attracted quite a lot of male attention, which did nothing to bolster *my* confidence. I kept my T-shirt on. I didn't need to be marked as inferior goods in the little comparison shopping game that was going on.

She offered me a pineapple daiquiri. She had two of them on the table beside her chair, one still untouched. They had been sent over by admirers. I declined, having no desire to hang around for Susan's leftovers, either drinks or men.

"One last afternoon of sun," she said, stretching luxuriantly. "I can't wait to get out of here tomorrow, though. Hopefully, I can turn the car in early. My flight out is at eight in the morning."

"What was the deal?" I asked. "Akito asking everyone to stay around for questioning?"

"I guess so. I don't know why. It sounds to me like he's got a pretty strong case against Mack Garvey."

I wondered who had told her that. There were still a lot of unanswered questions about Mack, and most of the so-called evidence was circumstantial.

Still, I felt no need to share my views with her.

She stared down toward her toes, flexing each leg muscle in turn, apparently admiring the way they looked. I wanted to open my notebook, but hesitated. I didn't especially want her there looking over my notes with me. I was trying to think of the best way to formulate the question about her unfinished health club, when she let out a little groan.

"Oh, shit, here comes the ice princess," Susan muttered under her breath.

I followed her line of sight, past the edge of the pool. Emerging from the small outdoor cafe under the colonnade was Catherine Page. She was walking straight toward us although she hadn't seen us yet.

"I am just not up for any of her bullshit," Susan said. "Excuse me."

She gathered her sunglasses, lotion, and wristwatch from the small table between us and strolled off in the opposite direction. Every male eye in the place followed her G-stringed rear end.

I wondered about her remark. I wasn't aware that she and Catherine Page even spoke, but apparently some pretty venomous words must have passed between them.

Catherine was almost even with my chair before she saw me. She wore a wide-brimmed hat and sunglasses I recognized as Dior. Her peach silk slacks and long-sleeved shirt gave her a tropical look, without exposing her delicate skin to the sun.

Once I knew she had seen me, it seemed rude not to acknowledge her, so I raised my fingers in a tiny wave.

"Oh, Charlie! How are you, dear?"

I wasn't aware that I rated being *dear* to her. I suspected this familiarity came from the Jack Daniels I could smell on her breath as she stretched out on the empty lounge to my right — not the one Susan had just vacated.

"Well, Catherine, will you be leaving the island tomorrow, too?" I asked.

"I suppose so," she sighed. "They sent Gil's body back yesterday, you know. I guess that means I have a funeral to plan."

She referred to it as though it were a charity function or an afternoon garden party, complete with silver tea service and tiny sandwiches. She didn't bother to pretend any grief over the occasion.

I tried to imagine her working up enough fervor to plot her husband's death. Perhaps the murder was something she had planned unemotionally, just as she would now plan the funeral.

"You know, if it weren't for the funeral and the fact that I miss Jason already, I wouldn't mind spending a little more time here." Her unfocused eyes scanned the pool area, and her voice got light and drifty again. "It's pleasant, you know."

She settled back into her chair and didn't seem to have much else to say. I obviously wasn't going to get my notes read with her sitting there, though, so I decided to pack it in.

I murmured something about reaching my limit with the sun, and pulled myself upright. I made sure my notebook was intact and reached to the small table on my left where I had set my room key.

Draped over the back of the chair Susan had occupied was a lime green jacket. It had to be hers; it matched her suit. Probably part of the expensive set I'd seen the receipt for several days ago.

I debated. If I left it there, it would probably end up in some backroom jumble of a lost and found, or some larcenous soul would recognize an expensive garment when they saw it and take it home with them.

At any rate, Susan would probably never get it back.

As little as I cared whether I saw her again or not, I knew the decent thing would be to return it to her. My mother had instilled these little courtesies somewhere in me. It would be easy enough for Drake and me to pop up to the tenth floor on our way out to dinner.

I picked it up, bade Catherine goodbye, and headed for the elevators.

Once in my room, I took a few minutes to update a couple of entries in my notebook. The motorcycle ride and my questioning of the boat rental guy seemed to have taken place days, rather than mere hours, earlier. I checked to be sure I had written down when I could find Willie Duran tomorrow. I had.

I stuck the notebook down in a side pocket of my purse and straightened up the room a little.

I chose a turquoise silk dress and gold sandals to wear to dinner then headed for the shower. The stinging hot water reminded me that my last shower had been at Drake's house this morning.

I wondered briefly where we would end up tonight.

13

Drake's knock on my door came promptly at seven. I wished I had thought to bring up something to offer as an hors d'oeuvre. We could always break into the mini-bar and see what it might offer. He looked me up and down appreciatively, admiring the way the turquoise silk fit.

"Would you like something to drink?" I offered, indicating the mini fridge.

"Maybe we ought to get going," he suggested. "Our reservation is for seven-thirty, and we have a way to go."

I picked up my purse, turned out all the lights but one, and peeked into the bathroom to make sure I'd put away my jewelry box. Didn't want to leave anything out that would tempt the night maid.

At the hotel entrance, Drake had the valet bring his truck around. The man held my door for me while Drake took the wheel. He steered around a concrete island, but at the driveway, instead of turning left and exiting to Rice Street, we turned right.

"Doesn't this lead to more of the hotel grounds?" I asked.

"We're going for a boat ride," he told me, a mysterious grin playing at the corner of his mouth.

He pulled into a large parking lot, not far away, and took my hand as we walked toward a small gray wooden building. As we passed through the breezeway, I could see a boat dock extending out into a narrow lagoon.

"The boats come along every fifteen minutes or so," he said, leading me to the water's edge. "I hope our timing will be about right."

"Is this a natural lagoon?"

"Nope. The whole thing is man-made. You won't believe how elaborate it gets."

He was right, I didn't.

Within minutes, I could hear the low throaty rumble of a boat engine. This one happened to be a mahogany launch made in Venice, according to the discreet brass placard near the steering wheel. I could tell it was expensive by the sound, rich and melodic, like a baritone doing a few warm-ups.

Half a dozen other people boarded with us, most of them making their way below deck where they could sit on thick upholstered cushions.

Drake and I opted to stay above, staking out a spot right on the rail. The captain steered his craft slowly, giving us plenty of time to ogle the scenery. Marble statues stood at tasteful intervals along the water's edge, illuminated by hidden lights which made them look as though they glowed from inside.

We passed under bridges that might have been on loan from Venice, and glided past fountains where leaping stone dolphins playfully sprayed water toward each other.

I found myself staring unabashedly, although I did make an effort not to let my mouth hang open. Behind us, a golden moon the size of a platter had just peeked over the mountains. Drake slipped his arm around my waist. I felt like the heroine in a mushy romance.

Now, *this* is what a vacation should be.

The captain skillfully steered the boat up to a pillared landing where a waiting crew member reached to take the ropes. We stepped out toward a small cluster of buildings, almost a mini-mall of shops.

Drake led me through the walkway, saying that the restaurant was just a little farther. Names like Armani, Rolex, and Lauren rolled past as we strolled through the arcade.

The restaurant was called Sharkey's and featured an eye-level tank, several hundred gallons large, where small live sharks swam in endless circles. Their gray and white bodies with the solid black eyes didn't look real to me. They seemed more like rubber toys, wound up to undulate around the bathtub.

"Are these from around here?" I asked.

"I don't know if this particular breed lives in our waters or not," Drake answered, "but we do have some sharks. You read about shark attacks in the paper all the time."

Hanging above the tank, suspended from the ceiling, was the taxidermied body of a great white shark. It was posed to stare down upon us, teeth exposed, ready to rip our guts out. I hoped our table would be out of sight of this ravenous creature. I wasn't sure he would help my appetite any. Large carnivorous sea creatures tend to make me squeamish. Drake's confirmation of real live sharks in the area made me glad that earlier I'd opted for the pool instead of the ocean.

A petite girl with dark curls down past her waist led the way to our table situated by the windows, looking out over the water.

The ground dropped away sharply outside. In the darkness below, I could see a faint hint of a narrow paved road and gently sloping ground. Based on the diorama I'd seen of the hotel grounds in the lobby, I guessed we must be directly above the golf course.

"The seafood here is great," Drake was saying. "I'm still a steak fan, despite what they say about red meat now, so I normally get the New York strip with lobster. But, everything on the menu is usually good."

I decided on the mahi mahi. Drake ordered scotch, and I settled for a daiquiri. I was really in the mood for a margarita on the rocks, but the waitress looked at me funny when I asked about it. Apparently, they made everything here in the frozen slushie machine.

Oh, well, nobody can make a margarita like my old buddy, Pedro, anyway. I'd just have to wait until I got home.

"So. Anything new on the case today?" Drake asked, once we had the preliminaries out of the way.

"I tracked down the name of the guard who was working the gate that night. Willie Duran. I'm planning on talking to him tomorrow."

"Willie's a local boy, young," he told me. "Not terribly ambitious, but he's got a little more on the ball than old Stanley."

"I read back through my notes this afternoon," I said. "When I came across the threatening letter we found on my windshield yesterday, it made me think of an angle I'd not considered before. Those words, 'let him fry.' That's pretty vindictive talk.

"What if Gil Page was killed specifically to implicate Mack? Is there anyone you can think of who hates Mack enough to do something like that?"

He stared out into the darkness for a couple of minutes. "I don't know, Charlie."

The fact that he didn't jump to an immediate denial made me wonder what was going on.

"Tell me what you're thinking, Drake."

"Oh, I don't know. It might not be anything."

He downed the last of his scotch and signalled the waitress to bring us both new ones. "There are lots of people who dislike Mack. It's the nature of the business here. These tour operators are so competitive that they're always at each other's throats. It's one of the main reasons I've never started my own operation here."

"Competitive enough to involve murder?" I asked.

He waited a minute until the waitress had set our drinks down and left.

"I honestly don't know. I know they have a constant series of court battles going on. They fight over the rights to landing pads, the locations of their landing pads, the flight routes, whether anyone is flying outside the voluntary noise abatement path . . . I could go on and on. They fight with each other, they fight with the state, they fight with the FAA."

I thought of the thick file marked Legal I'd found in Mack's office.

"Most of that sounds like it's verbal, though," I suggested.

"Mostly, it is. But, there have been a couple of cases where it got physical. Mack himself is one of the worst when it comes to stirring up the shit. He gets right in there and scraps with the best of 'em."

"Have there been any cases of serious revenge? Sabotage? Anything like that?"

"I don't think so. There seems to be some *gentlemen's code*, and I say that sarcastically because some of these guys are no gentlemen. I think if one of them were to sabotage another's equipment, it could start an all-out war. One thing would lead to another. Innocent lives would be lost. The lawsuits to follow would put everyone out of business overnight. No, even among the worst of them, I don't think anyone is quite willing to step over that line."

The two daiquiris had begun to go to my head, and I was glad to see the food arrive. As Drake had promised, everything was delicious. Conversation lagged for a few minutes as we both concentrated on matters of the stomach. The waitress checked on us once, then faded into the background.

"Drake, do you know anything about a legal battle between Mack and Bill Steiner?"

"Only that there is one. Mack complains about it all the time. Something about Steiner trying to overturn the airport management's decision to give Mack his landing pad. Steiner claims his name was on the list first, and he should have gotten the pad when it came available."

"Do you think it's a legitimate claim?"

"It really doesn't matter whether Steiner is legit or not," he said. "It will end up being an arbitrary decision made in court. Whoever loses will appeal and the fight will still be going strong until one of them runs out of money."

I didn't tell him it looked like Mack was quickly nearing that point.

"The only real winners will be the attorneys."

I chewed slowly on the last of my sourdough bread. So, what else was new?

The waitress came back then, and although I swore I couldn't hold another bite, Drake suggested that we split a dessert. It sounded tempting, hula pie.

When it arrived, I found out why it takes at least two people to eat it. In fact, one serving might have been suitable for a small dinner party. One "slice" of this pie was about the size of a small cantaloupe. Chocolate cookie crust, heaped high with macadamia nut ice cream, coated with thick fudge topping, trimmed out with whipped cream. We finished every bite.

I could see I was going to have to go against my instinctual dislike for exercise once I got home. I was getting a bad case of the five-pounds-heavier, vacation blues.

We lugged ourselves out of our chairs and retired to the patio area for an after-dinner Kahlua and coffee. The moon was high in the sky now, as shiny silver as a brand-new dime. It cast a streamer of white across the harbor, where we watched some late returning fishermen come in.

Drake held my fingers up to his lips and planted a slow sexy kiss on them that made my insides feel mushy.

It made me realize that the week was almost over.

I stared out across the water and wondered what it would be like to have a full-time man in my life. I think I'm too independent for most of them. In fact, one or two have admitted to being intimidated by me. But, this one was different. I sensed that he was secure enough that my self-sufficiency wouldn't bother him.

But, what would everyday life be like? I pictured his dirty socks abandoned on the floor, his shaving stuff in my medicine cabinet. He would probably come in and steal away Rusty's affections.

Maybe things were better this way. A few days of hot romance before getting back to real life.

The kisses were working their way across my forearm, past the bend in my elbow, headed toward my neck.

"Let's go back to your room," he whispered.

I was ready.

The slow boat ride back and the trip through the lobby and up the elevator did nothing to cool us off. I thought he would chew my left earring off by the time I located my room key.

I knew something was wrong the instant I unlocked the door.

The feeling came at me like a subtle change in the air, the way you know a few seconds in advance when it's going to rain.

Drake straightened abruptly, sensing my unease. I slowly pushed the door inward a couple of inches. I had left a light on but now the room was pitch black. I reached for the switches with my left hand, my right arm giving the door a hard shove.

The door banged back against the wall, as the room sprang into bright light.

14

We were alone.

It took a moment for my system to register what I saw. Nothing was as I had left it.

The mattress on the bed was askew, the covers pulled loose and left rumpled. My clothes in the closet had been roughly searched. Several items had fallen off their hangers and lay in small colorful heaps on the floor. The pocket of my linen jacket had one corner ripped loose. The drawers gaped in various stages of open, like uneven stairsteps. I felt violated, seeing my underwear strewn across the floor.

In the bathroom, my zippered makeup bag had been dumped. Jars and brushes were scattered across the vanity and into the sink. A lipstick and a mascara tube had rolled off and hit the floor.

Even the towels had been shaken out and thrown in piles in the tub and on the floor.

My sense of tidiness was outraged. For a person who is borderline fanatic about everything in its place, I saw this as the ultimate desecration. I wanted to cry, but my insides were shaking too hard.

Drake had followed me into the room. He stood now, as I did, obviously shaken by the chaos before us.

"We better call hotel security," he suggested in a quiet voice.

He stepped to the phone and punched some buttons. I stood in the middle of the room spotting some new travesty each place I looked. I had seen this happen to other people before. A former client's home had been robbed while I was working on her case, but this was the first time I'd experienced it myself. It's a whole different feeling when it's your own stuff.

"They'll be right here," Drake said, turning to me. "We shouldn't touch anything until they come."

It was all I could do to hold back. My fingers itched to begin refolding and putting away — to make order of the chaos an outsider had left. I didn't want a strange security man to see my bras hanging out of the drawers.

Drake put his arms around me. I allowed myself to press my cheek against his shoulder. His steadiness made me aware of my own trembling.

I still couldn't cry — I was too furious.

The knock on the door a few minutes later startled us both. Drake opened it to admit a man dressed in hotel uniform. His gold name tag said "M. Kanakoa, Security."

He stood somewhat over six feet, and weighed a little less than a Volkswagen. He had the solid neck and shoulders of a football player, but I could tell it had been a few years. The once-firm muscles had settled into softness, leaving him with more bulk than power.

His eyes scanned the room dispassionately. I might have imagined it, but I'd swear he checked first to see if the TV set was still there.

"What time did you folks go out tonight?" he asked.

"We left the room at seven," I said. My voice came out steadier than I thought it would. My insides were still tangled, while my head felt curiously light.

"And you just now got back?"

I nodded, wondering where he was leading. Did he honestly believe we'd sit here in this mess an hour or so before we decided to call and report it? I felt myself begin to get irritated.

He was examining the door, the lock, and the jamb. "Looks like they used a key."

"What time did the maids do turn-down service tonight?" I asked.

"I checked that. They were on this floor between eight and nine o'clock."

"So it had to have happened after that, or they would have reported it," I said.

"Not necessarily, ma'am," he said. He had a look on his face that basically said *Get Real*. "Some people's rooms always look like this."

Feeling properly put in my place, I turned to look around the room once again.

"Can you tell me if anything is missing?" he asked.

"I haven't touched a thing, yet," I told him. "We wanted you to see it just as we found it."

"I'll get someone up here to dust for fingerprints. In the meantime, you might as well be checking to see what they took. We can move you to a new room. Let me check with the front desk to see what's available."

"That's not necessary," I assured him.

The intruder probably hadn't been out to harm me, or he would have waited for our return. He had either found whatever he had searched the room for, or I didn't have it in the first place.

Kanakoa punched buttons on the phone, ordering the fingerprint kit brought up, and asked that a maid bring us fresh sheets and towels.

I started straightening the bathroom, replacing the spilled contents of my makeup bag one piece at a time. I couldn't see that anything was missing. The small hinged box containing a few pieces of costume jewelry appeared to be intact. I'd brought only three pair of earrings and one bracelet, none of them valuable. They were all there.

Drake gathered the disheveled towels and tossed them in a stack near the door. I worked quickly through the closet, hanging and straightening. Everything seemed to be there. Same with the dresser drawers.

My tote bag was on the floor near the dresser, and I could tell it had been rummaged through. Fortunately, my little spiral with all my notes about the case had been with me in my purse, along with the threatening note I'd found on my windshield. Nothing was missing.

In the meantime, a maid arrived.

Within five minutes she had fresh towels hanging in the bathroom and the bed was stripped and remade. As she gathered the old sheets, a tiny orchid fell on the carpet. So, the night maid had been here before the intruder.

I wasn't sure what significance that might have, but I tucked the fact into my mental file.

The fingerprint man came, dusted, and went. He exchanged a few words with Mr. Kanakoa, but none with me. I had the room in reasonable shape by then, and, while I hadn't counted every pair of panties, I was pretty sure nothing was missing.

What had they been after?

Granted, it could have been a hotel thief, after cash or valuables. If so, they obviously discovered that I travel light. But, something told me that wasn't what we had here.

A nagging sensation told me this had something to do with the murder of Gil Page.

I just wished I knew what.

15

Drake insisted on staying with me, although he said he would have to get up early since he was flying the next day. Truthfully, it didn't take a lot of argument on his part. Even with my little world back in order, something inside me didn't care for the idea of being alone just yet.

He held me close in the semi-dark room and didn't push for sex. It took my mind awhile to settle down enough to sleep.

When he left about five-thirty, I thought I'd go right back to sleep but it didn't work. I turned on the TV for the first time in a week and caught up on the world with CNN. Somewhere around the third time through Dollars & Sense, I drifted back off to sleep, waking again about nine.

I huddled beneath the warmth of the covers for a few minutes while my thoughts flicked in reverse sequence over the events of the last twenty-four hours. I felt a twinge of guilt that I was lying here doing nothing while Drake, who'd had even less sleep than I, was out there flying the circle, giving the tour.

I was twitchy to do something.

I picked up the phone, and called Pamela at the phone company. Remembering to identify myself as Catherine Page, I got the information I was after. Yes, there had been a call to Hawaii from the Page's home phone on Friday night.

Getting information on Catherine's airline schedule proved more difficult. Without official credentials, they weren't going to tell me anything. I decided I'd give it some thought. I might be able to figure out a way to bluff my way through.

If worse came to worse, I could tell Akito my suspicions, and he could check it out.

I headed toward the shower, wondering again about the break-in. Who was I getting close to?

The faces flashed through my mind, one at a time, but nothing made any sense.

I couldn't think of one shred of tangible evidence the intruder might think I had. My notes were possibly the only thing of value, and even then, why try to take them and leave me unharmed?

Or, maybe that was the next move.

Maybe I was close to something, and the killer intended to get rid of me next. I checked the deadbolt locks before I stepped into the tub.

The hot shower didn't help reconcile my mood.

I lathered my hair with shampoo, then stood under the spray, letting it course down my body. Fifteen minutes later, I was rubbing myself down with a fresh towel, feeling no better. I chose white cotton slacks and shirt from the closet and opened the drapes to let in the day.

Low clouds in clusters hung around the mountain tops. The water was slate blue and the palm trees below whipped in the wind with a sound like plastic pick-up sticks being shaken in a can. Although it was weak, enough sun hit the beach to bring out a good crowd. I opened the sliding glass door to let in the ocean breeze.

I closed my eyes and took a deep breath, willing my mind to clear.

I couldn't do it.

A low-grade anxiety ran through me like electromagnetic waves. I recognized the feeling. I had a mild case of it when I felt near the answer on my last case. This time I guess it was hitting me harder because my own turf had been invaded.

Maybe breakfast would help. I headed back to the bathroom to do something about my face and hair. I found my hairbrush and blow-dryer, and began work on getting my thick mop dry. Bending over at the waist, I aimed the dryer at the thickest hair, running the brush through it as I went. It's mindless work and I let my thoughts drift.

That's when I spotted something a little out of place.

It was a flash of silver, just under the edge of the drape next to the sliding glass door frame. The frame itself was dark metal, so what was the silver? I switched off the dryer and went to investigate.

There, in a spot we would have never seen last night, was a small object lying on the floor. I picked it up.

It was a fuse, the glass kind with silver at both ends. My mind flicked past a dozen little scenes.

The last time I'd seen any fuses was the day I talked to Joe Esposito in the hangar. He'd been cleaning up his workbench and had put several of them away in a small parts cabinet.

What had Joe Esposito been doing in my room, unless I was getting too close to something that involved him? And, how did he know I was getting close?

I tried to remember the conversations I'd had since I talked to Joe. Had I voiced my suspicions to anyone other than

Drake? Maybe I'd said something to Mack — or to Catherine? Even in my innocent inquiries with the old security guard, word might have got back to Joe that I was snooping around. I tucked the fuse into my pocket. Perhaps he had messed up my room to frighten me off.

Maybe robbery hadn't been the motive at all.

The discovery gave me renewed vigor. I wasn't about to cower in the corner, worrying over this. I went back into the bathroom, where I did a quick once-over with some blusher and lipstick. Grabbing my tote bag and purse, I headed downstairs.

"Ms. Parker!" My little buddy, Morton, beckoned me from behind the concierge desk. His voice dropped discreetly as I approached.

"I'm so glad I caught you. I was just trying to phone your room. Mrs. Catherine Page asked me to contact you."

His freckled hands fluttered nervously as he spoke, and I could have sworn his pink scalp was even pinker.

I had thought both Catherine and Susan were leaving today. Perhaps Catherine had thought of some new information for me.

"Mrs. Page is in the hospital." He was practically whispering now.

"What?"

"She was mugged last night," he said. "Right here in the hotel, although that is *not* public information. You didn't hear it from me."

Fine. Whatever. "You said she's in the hospital?"

"Kauai General. She asked us to get word to you. She would like to see you, if possible."

I thanked him, and said I'd get by to see her this morning. This certainly added a new wrinkle. I had planned on going right out to the airport to talk to Willie Duran, the security guard, but maybe I ought to see Catherine first.

I discovered her in a private room on the third floor. Cautiously, I entered, unsure what to expect. She was sitting up in bed, dressed in a filmy apricot peignoir with a border of down. The way it framed her face made her appear soft and delicate. There was a gauze square taped to her left temple, and beneath it an ugly purple bruise had begun spreading down her jaw.

Her eyes welled up at the sight of me. "Oh, Charlie," she said, her voice breaking on the last syllable. I submitted to a hug. The apricot feathers tickled my nose, almost triggering a sneeze reaction.

"What happened, Catherine?"

"I don't know exactly," she sniffed. "I came back to my room after dinner last night."

"What time was this?"

"Oh, about eight, I guess. Anyway, I walked into the room, and something near the bathroom door attracted my attention. I turned toward it, and that's the last thing I remember. Apparently, the night maid found me a few minutes later, and called the paramedics. I came to while they were working over me, but I felt so dizzy."

She must have been attacked about the same time my room was broken into. I had to believe it was all connected somehow.

But how?

And why?

"Do you know if anything was stolen from your room?" I asked.

"No, I was too out of it. I couldn't even stand up without feeling faint, much less check the room. One of the paramedics was a woman, and she got my gown and cosmetics case for me."

"I'm sure whoever was hiding in the bathroom was long gone by that time."

"Oh, yes. It all happened so fast I never even got a look at him."

She looked like she was about to cry again. Her hands trembled. I wondered whether it was from emotional trauma or the fact that she hadn't had a drink in several hours.

"Charlie, I was supposed to fly back to California this morning. I have to get back. Gil's funeral is tomorrow."

She touched the bandage gingerly. "I'm quite a sight, aren't I?"

"What has the doctor said about releasing you?"

"He checked me over this morning and said I could go any time. I'm just nervous about it. What if the person who hit me comes after me again? Charlie, can you help me find out who did this?"

I thought about that. I was supposed to be working for Mack, and I wasn't ready to tell Catherine that she was still one of my suspects. However, I felt certain that the mugging would tie in somehow to the rest of the case.

It also moved Catherine a little farther down the suspect list.

"I'll see what I can find out," I told her.

"Thanks." She looked relieved as she reached for a small leather case on the table beside the bed. I noticed again that her hands shook as she held a gold lighter to the tip of her cigarette.

Something was still bothering me, and I decided I wouldn't get anywhere unless I came right out with it.

"Catherine, what are your ties with Joe Esposito?"

She leaned back against her pillow and closed her eyes, taking a long pull on her cigarette. I sensed a debate going on inside. Finally, she exhaled deeply. Her eyes opened, but she kept them fixed on the ceiling.

"Joe thinks he's in love with me," she said.

Her voice became so quiet I had to practically lean over the bed.

"Three years ago, when Gil first loaned Mack the money for his business, we came over here to see the operation first-hand. Gil rarely involved me in his business deals, but I did go out to the heliport with him a time or two. I've never been brave enough to take a ride in one of those things, but they fascinate me.

"Joe was working on the helicopter and Mack introduced us. Joe's reaction to me was the weirdest thing. He acted like a star-struck groupie. I mean, he stared, he got flustered when I spoke to him, he told me he thought I was the most beautiful woman he'd ever seen. It was almost spooky. I've never had a man react to me like that — ever.

"A few days later, Mack and Gil had a meeting at our hotel, and Joe somehow managed to be invited along. I found it most disconcerting the way he stared at me. I was afraid Gil would notice. He was extremely possessive and insanely jealous. But, I guess Gil's mind was elsewhere because he never seemed to notice Joe."

"Did you ever see Joe alone?"

"No! I would have been frightened to, Charlie. His interest in me was almost fanatic."

"Did Joe ever show animosity toward Gil? Jealousy?"

"Not outwardly. Around Gil and Mack, he usually kept his eyes lowered, acting rather subservient."

"You said not outwardly. Did you see any indications privately?"

"Well, as I said, I really wasn't around him much. But, there was one time. I think it was during that meeting they all had at our hotel. Gil said something rude to me. I don't even remember what it was now, it was just his way. But, as I was leaving the room, I caught Joe staring at Gil with almost open hatred.

"I guess I remembered it because it was different from the
reaction most people usually had. When a man is rude to his
wife, most people will turn away, look embarrassed. I was
used to that. But Joe looked ready to jump to my defense. Sort
of a Latino machismo, you know."

I digested that. If Joe Esposito fancied himself in love with
Catherine Page, he might have taken it upon himself to
permanently fix her marital problems. Or, there was still the
possibility that Catherine and Joe had cooked up the plan
together. She might have implied favors to come if her husband was out of the way.

Right now, she seemed in control and sure of herself, but
I had seen her after a few drinks, too. Who knew what might
run through her head when she loosened up a bit?

However, those suppositions didn't help answer the question of who might have hit Catherine last night. Surely, Joe
wouldn't do that to the woman he said he loved? Unless, of
course, something in the little romance had gone awry.

Catherine was sitting up in bed now, looking better after
lightening her burden.

"Charlie, I need to get out of here. Could you help me get
checked out and take me back to the hotel?"

I wasn't really up for becoming her baby sitter, but I
supposed I could do at least that much. I told her to get dressed
while I walked down the hall to the nurse's station to see about
the paperwork. When I got back to her room with a wheel-
chair, which the hospital insisted on, Catherine was dressed.

She looked somewhat overdone in last night's attire, a
black cocktail dress with a gold lamé ruffle over one shoulder.
She had slipped on her black satin pumps without hose, and
her legs looked white and skinny with small blotches of
varicose veins showing.

She was still a little slow on her feet when we got to the
hotel, but made it to her room all right. I got on the phone to

see what could be done about changing her plane reservations, while she went into the bathroom and changed from her evening dress to a lightweight jogging suit. She gathered her few belongings and put them into her suitcase.

The soonest flight I could get for her didn't leave until seven that evening, so I suggested she use the time to sleep. After putting in a wake-up call for five-thirty, I told her to lock all the deadbolts behind me. I waited until I heard them click into place before walking off down the hall.

I felt increasingly uneasy as I walked out toward my car. The chat with Catherine had only solidified my nagging thoughts about Joe Esposito. Now I knew he had motive.

My next move would be to talk to Willie Duran. He should be able to confirm when Joe had come and gone from the hangar last Friday night. He might have even seen Joe removing the body.

That, coupled with the fuse found in my room, and Catherine's statement, might be enough to get the heat off Mack. The problem was still the disposal of the body. If I couldn't prove my boat theory, the suspicion would still be on Mack and his helicopter.

I felt like something was about to break, and I didn't like not knowing what it would be.

I was concerned, too, about Drake. If Joe really was our man, he could be dangerous. He must know we were getting close to something if he took the trouble to ransack my room last night. He must know, too, that Drake and I were involved with each other. If Joe wanted Drake out of the way, it would be a simple matter for him to sabotage the aircraft.

I thought of the miles of treacherous coastline where an emergency landing would be difficult, if not impossible.

I drove slowly past the helipads. Mack's helicopter was out. It didn't ease my mind any. I parked near the maintenance area, locked the car and approached the gate.

Willie Duran was a cocky little rooster of a man, twenty-eight or -nine, his black hair slicked back on the sides, low in front like a young Elvis. He watched me approach the gate with an appreciative gleam in his eye, like I was doing a strip-tease just for him. I guess his attitude was supposed to be a turn-on, but it's not my style.

He wore his uniform about a size too small, so it fit like a glove. The short sleeves of his shirt were rolled up several turns to impress the world with his biceps. Sleazy. I thought of the poor girl staying home with kids hanging all over her.

"Hey, doll," he said, "what can I do for you?" His voice was low and he probably meant it to sound provocative.

Doll is among the list of names, including honey, baby, and sweetie, which I do not take well to. I felt myself becoming cool, if not downright frosty. I pulled out my card and note-book, not bothering to explain the limits of my duties with the investigation firm. His puffed-out pectorals dropped percepti-bly when I didn't warm up to his bait.

"I have some questions for you pertaining to last Friday night. I understand you were on duty that night from three to eleven?"

His weight shifted from one foot to the other; his flashy smile disappeared. I could tell he was discomfited dealing with a woman in authority. I loved it.

"Is that correct?" My voice sounded sharp but I wasn't going to cut this creep any slack.

"Uh, yes, ma'am."

Ma'am. That's more like it. "You are aware that a man was murdered that night, over in the Paradise Helicopters han-gar?"

"Yes, ma'am. The police, they already been here."

"I'm representing an innocent man who is under suspicion. I may have to ask some of the same questions over."

He nodded, peering toward my notebook. I tilted it away from him. Nosy little jerk.

"How did the victim get into the hangar? Did he have a security badge?"

"Well, he walk up to the gate with Mack Garvey. I stop him, and ask to see his badge, but Mack say it's okay. I tell him I'm supposed to see a badge, but Mr. Garvey get real irritated. It was late and no one around, so I went ahead and let them both go through."

"Was Joe Esposito around?"

"His truck was in the lot. Been there all afternoon."

"Was Joe in the hangar when the other two arrived?"

"I don't know. He goes back and forth between the hangars a lot. He does maintenance for Mack, for Bill Steiner, some others, too, so he's all over the place."

"Did he leave during the evening?"

He shuffled a little and avoided eye contact. "I'm not sure. Most times he takes a dinner break, but I can't remember if he did that night."

"After Mack and his visitor got here, did you hear an argument between them?"

He grinned. "There's so much noise around here, I don't notice. You know, planes taking off and landing, helicopters, the wind, the surf."

It was probably a dumb question. Even standing three feet apart, we were having to raise our voices slightly just to converse. But Joe had said he overheard the argument. It was worth asking.

"Willie, did you see Mack and the visitor leave? Either or both of them?"

Again, the lack of eye contact. "Nope. Neither one."

"How could that be? Mack says he had an argument with the other guy, then he got mad and left. How could he have got past you without your seeing him?"

He shrugged.

I watched him shift from one foot to the other. His eyes darted around, connecting everywhere except with my gaze, which I kept steadily on his face.

"Willie . . . you left your post that night, didn't you?"

"Look, don't tell, please." The cockiness was all gone. I was looking at a scared overgrown teenager. I waited for him to continue.

"Clarissa, that's my girlfriend, she came by that night. She was crying and carrying on, said she had to talk to me. Said she just found out she was pregnant, and what were we going to do about it.

"I had to get her out of here. I got a wife and kids at home, too. I had to calm Clarissa down before she did something stupid."

A girlfriend? Wow, he *was* a busy little dude.

"I took her back to her car, and we drove down to Ahukini Landing. It's only a quarter mile or so away, but at least it's private. I was only gone maybe a half hour."

"Did you lock the gate when you left?"

"I think so, but I'm not really sure. I was busy worrying about where I was going to come up with abortion money, when my wife takes every paycheck of mine straight to the bank."

He looked like he might burst into tears.

"Look, I can't let Jack Akito find out about this. His wife and mine are cousins. He'd kill me."

I almost felt sorry for the little jerk. How do people manage to get themselves into these things? I wondered if he had ever considered the merits of keeping his pants zipped.

I left him standing there looking considerably less sure of himself than he'd been when I arrived.

16

Back in my car, I looked at my watch. It was still only two o'clock. Drake wouldn't be through with his last flight until around five. A glance at the date told me that, unless I changed my plans, I only had two more days here on the island. I really should buy some gifts to take back home.

Besides, distancing myself from the case for a few hours might help snap something into perspective that was still missing.

Willie had told me that Joe did maintenance for both Mack and Bill Steiner. Could Joe somehow be involved in their legal scrapping? If he had a grudge against Mack, that would certainly be one way to fuel the fire. I wondered how I could find out more about the ongoing battle.

I had started the car and put the gearshift in reverse when I heard the distinctive boom-boom-thud, boom-boom-thud of a stereo behind me. Joe Esposito's top-heavy looking red pickup truck was just pulling into the lot. He parked two spaces down from me and cut the engine. I backed out and headed back toward the road.

As I drew even with his truck, I felt him watching me. When I looked out at him, he quickly averted his eyes.

The little glass fuse down in my pants pocket rubbed against my leg.

Joe walked on past me without a backward glance. In my rearview mirror, I saw him present his security badge to Willie Duran and pass through the gate. Willie said something to Joe and they both looked up at me.

The Mack Garvey/Bill Steiner question continued to nag at me. Here was one man who made no secret of the fact that he'd like to put Mack out of business.

Seeing that Mack went off to jail would be a quick and inexpensive way to do it. A lot less expensive than a legal battle.

I debated whether to try to track Steiner down and question him. Assuming I could, though, what would I ask him? *Hey, Bill, ever think about killing some guy you don't know, just to put one of your competitors out of business?*

Somehow, I didn't think I'd get too far with that.

The traffic light at Ahukini and Kuhio took forever to turn green, but I finally got my chance. I was wandering, I had to admit, a little at a loss for what to do next, halfway looking for somewhere to buy a few tourist goodies.

On my right, I suddenly noticed the newspaper office just ahead. On an impulse, I pulled into the parking area, almost getting rear-ended in the process.

If they had copies of back issues, I might be able to find something about Steiner's and Mack's lawsuit. Mack's file only presented one side of it. I wondered if the battle had ever made the local news.

On the outside, the newspaper office looked about the same as many other small businesses on the island — cinderblock building with peeling paint, weeds growing up through cracks in the parking lot. Inside, though, it was clean and well-lit. A half-dozen people worked at computer terminals.

The girl at the front desk had skin the color of toffee and straight black hair that was so long I wondered how she avoided sitting on it.

She showed me to the microfiche reader and demonstrated how to work it. I asked to see the issues from one to two years old.

According to Mack's file, the lawsuit had started about a year ago. I hoped to find something immediately before that time that might have precipitated it.

Steiner's name wasn't difficult to locate. He was obviously one of the more vocal helicopter operators on the island, frequently quoted on one issue or another. I went back fourteen months, and didn't find anything linking his name to Mack's. I kept looking.

Another month or more passed with no mention of either name. When I next came across Steiner's name, I stopped with a jolt.

Steiner had been arrested fifteen months ago for assault and battery on one Gilbert Page.

According to the article, the California tourist, Page, had become verbally abusive after having a few too many at a local night spot. Apparently, an exchange had begun between the two men, the subject of which was the cocktail waitress who had served them both.

The argument had ended with Page out cold on the floor and Steiner being escorted to the drunk tank.

I flipped the film back a few more days, but there was no further mention of the incident. I wondered whether it truly was a random bar fight or if Gil and Steiner had known each other?

Even so, I wasn't sure how this new twist would help Mack. It still didn't alter the fact that Mack had admittedly been one of the last to see Gil alive, or that no one had yet brought Steiner's name into the picture. None of the people who had been around the maintenance hangar that night had placed Steiner there.

Once again, I considered tracking Steiner down and questioning him. Again, I couldn't seem to formulate questions that would make much sense.

I switched off the microfiche reader and thanked the girl for her time.

Back in my car, I debated where to go next. Without a better plan, I headed toward a little shopping area near the hotel to look for gifts for those back home. The various implications of the case roared around in my head, not solving anything, but not leaving me alone either.

Finding a parking space at the small mini-mall of shops took about ten minutes — three passes through the parking lot before someone vacated a spot. I took advantage of their leaving, cutting off a sports car full of college kids.

Situated in a center courtyard around which the twenty or thirty shops held ranks, I located a cluster of pay phones. I dialed Bill Steiner's helicopter company, realizing that he would probably be out on a flight. To my surprise, the receptionist put me right through to him. I briefly introduced myself and my purpose.

"I ain't talkin' to no one who's workin' for Mack Garvey," his voice informed me harshly. "Talk to my lawyer."

"Wait!" I paused to be sure he hadn't hung up. "I just wanted to ask a quick question or two — not about Mack." I rushed the words out.

He didn't say anything, which I took as a go-ahead.

"Did you know Gil Page before the night you got into the fight with him in the bar?"

"Huh? Look, lady, I don't know *what* the hell you're talkin' about."

"Never mind." I thanked him and hung up. I believed him. And I'd known the theory was far-fetched.

My hand rested on the inert phone receiver, my eyes staring out at nothing for a full three minutes, until I realized that a woman was waiting to use the phone.

"Sorry." I turned away.

I spent the next hour at the crowded little tourist trap, stocking up on goodies to take home with me. Kona coffee for Mrs. Higgins, macadamia nut chocolates for Ron— although he certainly doesn't need them, ball caps for his three kids. I also picked up a dozen postcards. If I mailed them this after-noon, they'd probably arrive in New Mexico within a week after I did.

I strolled through a couple of the other shops in the little strip where I bought the treats, admiring the silks and hand painted clothing, wondering whether I should get myself a little something, too.

Halfway down the row, I paused before a window, staring but not seeing.

Holy shit, I thought. How blind could I have been?

The mannequin in the window was wearing a lime green bikini with the matching jacket. *That's* what was missing from my room last night.

I'd never returned Susan's jacket to her as I intended, but it wasn't there after the break-in.

I froze to the spot, my mind dancing.

What was the connection? Susan didn't know I had the jacket. But, Catherine did. She had seen me take it from the pool, although I hadn't said anything to her about it. She would have probably assumed it was mine.

And, what about Joe? If he had dropped the fuse from the maintenance hangar in my room, why did he take the jacket? What about his professed love for Catherine?

If he thought he was protecting her, how did the jacket fit in?

I had absentmindedly watched Catherine pack her suitcase this morning. If the green jacket had been among her things, surely I would have noticed it.

And how did Catherine's mugging tie in with the demolition of my room and the theft of the jacket?

There were too many questions without answers, and it was beginning to make my head hurt.

I headed back to the Westin. At the front desk, they informed me that Susan Turner had checked out early this morning. Catherine Page had not left yet. It was only three-thirty. She had left her wake-up call for five-thirty, so I assumed she would still be asleep.

In my room, I sat down to write out a few postcards. My thoughts refused to settle down, though, and I ended up writing a few lines of banality on each. I did write a brief paragraph about Drake to Elsa Higgins.

Within a few minutes, I had the postcards finished and was feeling restless. I thought about Steiner and the fact that he'd had at least one blowup with Page. But would that provide motive for a murder almost a year and a half later? I doubted it. His apparent confusion when I'd mentioned Page's name made me believe that he didn't even remember the incident.

Catherine's admission this morning that Joe was in love with her kept tugging at my attention. It certainly gave Joe a strong motive. Especially if he got wind of the reaming out Gil had given Catherine over the phone that same evening. He said he'd overheard the discussion between Gil and Mack. I paced to the balcony. The fresh wind calmed me only slightly, and I turned back inside.

Maybe Gil's phone conversation with Catherine had come to light. One by one, the puzzle pieces were beginning to come together. The answer was here, close.

I needed to talk to Joe, to see his reaction to my new knowledge. But, the man intimidated me and I didn't relish confronting him alone. If I waited until Drake was through flying, maybe he'd go with me.

The late afternoon sun shone from under gray clouds and hit my glass door in a pink-gold shaft. I might still be able to find Joe at the heliport. There should certainly be people around, in case of trouble. I could always call Akito and tell him my theory. Somehow, though, I didn't think he would welcome it. He was still set on the idea that Mack was the guilty man.

Until I had proof, I'd rather leave him out of it.

Pacing around the room wasn't helping , though. I had to do something. I closed the drapes and left a light on, then made sure I had securely locked the door. The elevator seemed to take forever, adding to my sense of urgency.

Outside, the sky had an eerie twilight feel to it. Although the sun wasn't quite down yet, the clouds had thickened considerably. I put the top up on the car, started it, and headed out to Rice Street.

Traffic was heavy, people rushing to get home at the end of a long day. I left most of them behind when I made the turn toward the airport.

I cruised slowly past the pads at the heliport. All the helicopters were in, lined up in a neat row, their rotor blades tied down for the night.

All except Drake's ship.

I glanced at my watch. Surely, he should have been in by now. The thread of anxiety which had run loosely through me all day cinched itself into a tight knot.

The maintenance hangar looked quiet — too quiet. The helicopter wasn't there, nor was Joe's red pickup truck. I didn't like the feel of it. The puzzle pieces that had eluded me all afternoon suddenly fell into place. My gut clenched as I realized the killer had probably gotten away.

Where was Drake?

The clouds which had earlier gathered in clumps over the mountains now spread into an even layer covering the sky like a heavy gray camping tarp. The wind whipped bits of debris across the ramp, the chain link fence catching the biggest part of them. A ripped potato chip bag flew past my ankles as I got out of the car. I shoved my purse under the seat, slipping my car keys into my pocket.

The guard was not in his enclosure, and the gate was standing wide open. Something wasn't right. I remembered seeing a phone in the maintenance hangar. If I could get inside, I would call Paradise's office to see if Drake had radioed in.

The walk-in door was closed, but as I got nearer, I noticed the big sliding doors stood open about a foot. I felt a spatter of rain as I approached them and heard thunder in the distance. Inside, the hangar was dark except for a single fluorescent fixture suspended over the workbench.

My flat loafers made hollow sounds as I walked across the empty room, like a premonition of danger in a scary movie. The background music usually gets intense at that point. I tried to tiptoe, but the shoes only slipped off my heels, making more noise than ever.

What was I so jittery for?

The telephone sat on the bench. It was so encrusted with greasy fingerprints, I couldn't tell what color it had been originally. I looked down at my clothes. White had not been a good color choice. How many hours ago had I gotten dressed? I reached for the slimy receiver. Bringing it near my face almost made me choke.

Luckily, I remembered the phone number for Paradise.

"Paradise Helicopters," Melanie answered. Did I imagine a high-pitched edge to her voice?

"Melanie, it's Charlie. Is anything wrong?"

"Oh, hi, Charlie. I don't know . . . I can't raise Drake on the radio, and he's already thirty minutes late."

"I'm at the maintenance hangar and nobody is here; at least I can't see anyone. Is Mack around?" I found myself trying to sound normal, not wanting to let her edginess get to me.

"No, he had a meeting with his attorney. He's been gone all afternoon." She sounded about ready to cry.

"What's your normal procedure in a case like this?" I asked. My own voice sounded shaky to me, and I forced myself to slow down. No sense in both of us going into a panic.

"I don't know. Nothing like this has ever happened before," she whined.

"Okay, Melanie, calm down. We have to think. Do you have a list of emergency phone numbers there somewhere?"

I heard a lot of paper-crinkling noises before she answered. "You mean like the FAA, the control tower, those kind of numbers?"

"That would be good for a start anyway. Also, why don't you try . . . "

"Put the phone down. He's not coming back." The harsh voice behind me made me jump, sending my heart crashing loudly into my ribcage.

I carefully lowered the receiver, placing it on its cradle at an angle so I wouldn't break the connection. I prayed that ditzy Melanie would have enough smarts to realize I was in trouble. I turned slowly, shielding the telephone with my body.

Susan stood about ten feet from me, gripping a wrench almost the size of Delaware.

She was wearing her green jacket.

Susan. She hadn't left the island after all. I wasn't sure whether to feel relieved or terrified.

Why, until a few minutes ago, hadn't I seriously considered her as a suspect? Because she had seemed so broken up over Gil's death? Because her alibi had checked out?

"Why isn't Drake coming back, Susan?" I raised my voice slightly, hoping Melanie was getting all this.

"Sugar in the gas tank," she answered. "I had to get rid of him." She laughed derisively at me. "*You*, miss smart-ass detective, you don't know anything. Your fly-boy lover was closer to figuring it out than you were."

That stung. Especially since I didn't know what the heck she was talking about. I wasn't about to give her the satisfaction of asking, so I let her continue.

"I was almost out of here twice now, and didn't make it because that creep screwed it up. The day after I killed Gil, I planned on getting out right away. I figured no one would find his body where I left it. Then Drake changed his flight pattern, and the whole mess came to light. I was really pissed when the cops wouldn't let me leave.

"I hung around here for days of questions, being as cool as I could about it, until I finally got my chance this morning. I'm booked on the first flight out, and I'm loading my stuff into the car when your lover comes out to the parking lot. I couldn't believe it. His truck was parked right next to me.

"I could tell, the minute he said hello, that something went off in his head. He stared at my rental car, and I knew he'd made the connection. If Gil drove the rental car out to the hangar to meet Mack on Friday night, how did the car get back to the hotel parking lot Saturday morning for me to use? He didn't say anything, but I knew that he knew."

"So, why didn't you head straight for the airport this morning and beat it out of here?"

"And be hauled back here the minute he told his story? No way. Plus, I wasn't sure how much you knew. For all I knew, once you figured out my jacket was the only thing missing from your room, I was probably the subject of your pillow talk last night. I followed you around all morning, but never could catch you alone.

"After awhile, I figured that you really didn't know, or else you would have run straight to the police. I came back out to the heliport and watched for my chance. Paradise apparently didn't have an early afternoon flight booked, because Drake didn't come right back after lunch. I waited until no one was paying attention and sneaked out to the helicopter. I figured some sugar in the fuel tank would do the trick."

I remembered Drake telling me about using autorotation to bring the aircraft down safely. There was still hope, but I wasn't going to tell Susan.

Susan was swinging the heavy wrench up and down, smacking it softly into the palm of her left hand. I had to keep her talking.

"So, you broke into my room to get your jacket back. Why? Wouldn't it have been simpler to just ask me for it?"

"I couldn't take the chance that you might've looked through the pockets. If you had, you'd know that there was a cashier's check in there for a quarter mil."

"Whoa! Two hundred fifty thousand, spendable?"

"Gil had given it to me our first night here. The money was for me to get my health club built. You almost had me there, too, you know. When you got back from California, I was surprised you didn't say anything about it."

Why hadn't I? Oh yes, Catherine Page had walked up and a distracted Susan had beaten a hasty retreat from the pool.

"You carried a huge cashier's check around in your *pocket*? Why didn't you keep it in the hotel safe?"

"Gil might have been able to get it back," she answered.

I kept stalling. "You could have mailed it back to California. I don't know, Fed Ex or something."

She shifted from one foot to the other, a tiny crease of uncertainty appearing between her brows. It didn't matter at this point anyway. I just needed to keep her talking.

"So, if you had the money, why did you have to kill Gil?"

"To keep it. Remember, I told you he and Catherine had argued terribly over the phone. Well, toward the end of that fight, I heard him tell her that he would get the money for Jason's race car from another source. I knew that other source was either Mack Garvey or me. It made me so mad to hear him give in to Catherine like that, I told myself he wouldn't get the money back from me."

"So you went with him to the hangar?"

"Yeah. I offered to ride out there with him, to kinda calm him down after the fight with Catherine. He thought I was being considerate."

"But the hotel verified that you ordered a movie in your room."

"All you have to do with those pay-per-view movies is turn on the TV set to the right channel. They automatically bill you for the movie. So, as Gil and I were leaving, I switched on the TV, and hung out the 'Do Not Disturb' sign. I told him I wanted it to look like we were in, in case the maid came around. We had parked near one of the hotel's side entrances, so we didn't walk out through the lobby. No one saw us leave, and no one saw me return two hours later."

"So, you came to the hangar with him, and waited for your chance."

"We drove up and parked. I told Gil I'd wait for him in the car. Mack Garvey came pulling in about then, but he parked at the other end of the lot and didn't see me. Gil and Mack walked up to the gate about the same time and the guard let them in. Then the place really started hopping. Some girl drove up and went over to talk to the guard. I couldn't hear what they were saying, but she looked real upset, and he finally steered her back to her car, and the two of them drove off.

"I was in a dark part of the lot and they didn't see me sitting in my car. They were no sooner gone than I saw that mechanic who works for Mack. The one that always looks like he has a burr up his rear. He came walking around the side of the hangar, and when he got to the door, he stopped. He looked like he was listening to whatever was going on inside for awhile, then he beat it out to the parking lot and took off in his truck."

So Joe had told the truth.

"I thought I better find out for myself what was going on. The mechanic hadn't pulled the gate tight, so I walked on up to the hangar and stood near the door so I could see through a little crack and hear what was going on. Gil and Mack were going at it. Finally, Mack told Gil flat out that he didn't have any money. If Gil wanted to take the helicopter, fine, he'd have to take it by force. Mack just turned around and walked out, leaving Gil standing there. I ducked into a dark shadow just before he came outside.

"By then, I realized it's now or never. Gil was going to try to get the money from me, since Mack didn't have any. I slipped into the hangar. He had his back turned, and it was a simple matter to pick up the handiest heavy object and whack him with it."

"But, once he was dead, wasn't he heavy? How'd you move him?" I thought I heard a police siren in the distance, but I couldn't be sure.

The wind had picked up, whistling through the rusted holes in the old metal building. I didn't like the way she swung the wrench a little more firmly as she got closer to the end of her story.

Susan looked at me scornfully. "Heavy? I can bench-press two hundred pounds," she said. "His size made it a little awkward, but the weight was nothing."

Nothing. Sure. I wanted to slap the smirk off her face, but I didn't want to break my hand doing it. I really *was* going to have to start working out — if I made it out of here in one piece.

"So, how did you get him out to the Na Pali? Or, is flying helicopters another of your many talents?"

Again, I thought I heard a siren, but the wind blew the sound away. Rain was beginning to drum on the metal roof, and we both raised our voices to be heard.

"I wasn't sure at first what I'd do with him," she said. "I hadn't planned that far in advance. But, I knew it had to be somewhere that people wouldn't find him right away. We had taken one of those snorkeling trips earlier in the week, and I knew there were lots of rugged valleys out there.

"I drove out to the end of the road, thinking I'd carry him partway up the trail, then take him off to the side somewhere. But, I got luckier than that. Some fool had left a small motor boat pulled up on the beach. There were no cars around, and no one camping, so I just borrowed the boat for a little while. I worked fast. It didn't take long at all to motor over to the first deep valley and beach the boat. I carried him as far inland as I could, and dumped him behind a boulder. I figured wild animals would get him before anyone found him."

"So, you put the warning note on my windshield? And what about Catherine? Did you knock her over the head last night, too?"

"When I realized I'd left my jacket at the pool, I almost panicked. I went back to look for it, but you and she and the jacket were gone. I searched her room first, and she was just unlucky enough to walk in about two minutes too soon."

There was a slight pause in the falling rain, and the siren sound came through distinctly. This time, Susan heard it too. She changed instantly from her talkative self-congratulatory mood, to one of near panic. Her eyes grew wide, and I could see perspiration glistening on her upper lip.

"Well, Charlie, looks like I need to get going. After killing Gil and Drake, you don't honestly think I'd let you get away, especially now that you know the whole story."

I supposed that would be asking a bit much. I watched her fingers grip the wrench tighter.

Her actions started happening in slow motion, as my brain took its time assimilating the situation. Her right arm, wrench outstretched, swung out to its full extension. She closed the gap between us with a quick little two-step as she swept the wrench in a downward arc aimed at my skull. I tried to leap backward, but the workbench bumped the middle of my back, blocking my way. I managed to duck, bent at the waist.

I dove for the floor behind her.

Her weapon came down hard on the edge of the wooden workbench. The impact should have dislocated a person's shoulder, but not Susan's. However, the element of surprise did cause her fingers to let go. The heavy wrench made sparks when it hit the floor. It skated across the concrete like it was greased.

We both scrambled for it but she got there first. I backed off and scanned the area for something I could use that might help my odds.

Nothing I could see was a match for Susan's arm wielding fifteen pounds of metal.

I decided distance was my best bet. I side-stepped out of range, trying to work my way toward the door.

Susan might be all muscle, but she was also fast. She made an all out run toward me, closing the distance quickly. I could see her arm raised in preparation for another swing, so I turned and bolted for the door.

It was pitch dark outside now, and the drenching rain made visibility almost nil. Lights from the other buildings and from the guard's post were blurred into uselessness. There were so many reflections on the slick tarmac that I couldn't distinguish anything. I couldn't see the guardhouse or the gate.

I didn't have time to debate the question either.

I took off in the direction that felt right. I could hear Susan right behind me and half expected the wrench to come down across my shoulders at any second, ending it all.

The guard's enclosure and gate gradually came into blurry view as I ran as fast as I could. I couldn't tell whether the guard was back at his post yet, but the gate looked shut as I got closer to it. Let it not be locked, I begged silently.

Water ran down my face and a strand of wet hair glued itself across my left eye. I wanted to brush it aside, but didn't dare lose my concentration that long.

As I reached for the gate knob, I thought I saw a flash of welcome blue police light, somewhere beyond the parking lot. It came too late, though.

Susan caught up with me as I pulled the gate open. She didn't take the time to aim well, or she would have killed me.

As it was, I felt a bone-jarring blow to the side of my head.

The light-reflecting raindrops got brighter as my legs went rubbery. Something inside told me that she would put me down permanently with one more blow. I gripped the chain link gate for support, and kicked toward her with the little force I had left.

I made contact, but it didn't feel solid. I heard the wrench clatter against the tarmac, and then there were sirens.

Nice, close sirens.

17

I came to, to the sounds of foreign voices, the throb of the world's worst headache, and the smell of wet hair. I was lying on the tarmac, half in and half out of the guard's enclosure. I guess they had dragged my top half under cover so I wouldn't drown while lying there. I felt like I'd been thrown, completely clothed, into a cold shower.

My clothes were wet clear through to, and including, my underwear. My hair clung to the side of my face, exacerbating the pain from my wound. I wanted to curl up and go to sleep, warm and dry, for a few days.

Mostly, I would settle for being dry.

No one seemed to be paying particular attention to me as I dragged myself to a sitting position. Every part of me was cold and stiff, and I wondered how long I had been there.

I held my head steady with both hands as I tried to assess the situation. Warm liquid ran down my neck, behind my right ear. When my fingers came away sticky I realized it was blood. I pressed the heel of my hand against the spot.

A wave of dizziness swept over me. I lowered my head between my knees while trying to keep pressure on the wound. I tried to remember everything I knew about head injuries, but found I was having trouble remembering where I was. After a minute, I gave it up.

Blue patrol car lights filled the air. They hurt my eyes, but there was nowhere I could turn to avoid them. Water-covered surfaces bounced the lights everywhere.

Two officers were leading Susan, handcuffed, toward one of the cars. Fuzzy radio transmissions blurred with the voices around me until I could no longer tell how many were speaking or what they were saying. Finally, an officer approached me.

"I don't know if you should be sitting up," he said gently. "We've called an ambulance for you."

"It's okay." My words sounded slurred, even to me. "Where's the helicopter?"

He looked like he didn't understand me at first. "Oh, the helicopter that was reported missing?"

I nodded once. Pain, hot as an electric shock, shot into my head. My stomach lurched.

"They found it," he said. "I hear it's going to need some serious work, but the pilot and passengers are all okay. They're bringing them in from Waimea now."

The ambulance attendants approached and noticed the blood on my hand. The bleeding had pretty much stopped, but they applied a pressure bandage just to be sure. I didn't want them to put me on a stretcher, but I had to admit that being wrapped in a blanket felt wonderful. I found myself getting the shakes. It's times like this I want my mommy. I let myself doze off once the ambulance started moving.

At the hospital, I let them do whatever they wanted. I lay submissively while various people shone lights into my eyes, ears, nose, and throat, and X-rayed my head from several angles. The doctor was a soft-spoken Japanese man with close cropped hair, gold wire-rimmed glasses, and warm hands.

"You're a lucky girl," he said, after tying off the last of the sutures. "Nothing's broken, amazingly. If she'd gotten a better swing at you . . . well, it could have been serious."

Yeah, like dead.

"I'd like to keep you overnight for observation," he continued, "but I don't want you going to sleep for a few hours yet. I know your greatest wish right now is probably for a nice long nap, but with a head injury, we want to see you up and around a bit first."

"I can't see much point in staying in the hospital if I can't go to sleep. I'd rather go back to my room where at least I'll have a comfortable bed and a change of clothes."

"Not unless you have someone to keep an eye on you through the night. You'll need to be wakened every few hours to make sure you are coherent."

"I'll do it," Drake's voice came from the doorway. He came to my bedside and hugged me gently. Raising my head from the pillow sent another jolt through my skull.

"Drake, you don't have to do that," I protested. "I'm used to taking care of myself. I can set an alarm clock."

"No way." He motioned the doctor out into the hall, where they conferred.

I wanted to be irritated that they were talking about me as though I were a child, but frankly, I was just too tired. I felt my eyes slipping shut. Okay, maybe I could let myself be pampered just this once.

"Charlie, wake up, hon." Drake's voice spoke softly near my ear.

I mumbled something blurry, realizing I'd drifted off to sleep in the hospital bed.

"The doctor says I can take you home," he continued. "Unless you'd rather be admitted for the night here."

"No, no." I raised up on one elbow. The pain was slightly less excruciating than it had been earlier. "Definitely not here."

My clothes were still laying in a soggy puddle in the corner of the room, so the nurse suggested that I wear the hospital gown and robe. Drake gathered my few possessions and guided my hand toward the release form. My fingers didn't cooperate very well but I did manage a shaky signature.

"Your place or mine?" he asked once we were in his truck.

"I need some clean clothes." My voice and my thoughts were becoming a little clearer. "Drake?"

"Um hmm," he answered, starting the truck and backing out of the parking slot.

"Did you really figure out this morning that Susan was the killer?"

"What?"

"She told me you saw her in the hotel parking lot this morning, and that you looked right at her and at her rental car, and that you knew she killed Gil."

"Well," he chuckled, "she gives me a lot more credit than I deserve. I noticed her this morning, but the only reason I stared at the car was because it was exactly like your rental. It took me a minute to realize that she wasn't getting into your car."

I reached out to squeeze his forearm. "Thanks," I mumbled. Then I drifted off to sleep again.

18

I'm settling into my window seat for my fourth crossing of this same two thousand miles of ocean in the past ten days. The fourteen stitches at the base of my skull are neatly hidden now by my hair, but my head is throbbing slightly. I'm about ready to pop one of my pain killers and drowse the night away.

The vacation was a good one — interesting, if not restful; eventful, if not relaxing. Drake cushioned my last two days by taking me home with him and providing a hot shower, fresh clothes, and homemade soup. He even brought me a box of chocolates, and kissed me goodbye at the airport — all the stuff women find romantic, and men rarely provide. Drake Langston is a unique man.

I find myself thinking about him now. As the plane is pushed back from the jetway, I can see his silhouette against the backlit windows. One hand is raised, tentatively, it seems.

If I could see his facial features, I imagine there would be a wistfulness around the eyes.

Last night we talked — personal stuff, plans. I tried to keep the mood light, to avoid making this whole encounter take on more significance than it should. Drake wanted so much to fall in love with me, and I must admit, the idea was tempting. But wasn't this really just a shipboard romance, a wild, fun, fleeting thing?

He had asked me when I could come back. I told him I couldn't foresee it anytime soon. I asked him when he might come to the mainland. He wasn't sure. I felt any definite plans fizzling. And yet, there was something more. Even with my head bandaged, my color lousy, and my speech dopey with pain medication, Drake looked at me with such tenderness, with a caring and, yes, a love, no one had ever shown me before.

I glanced back at the terminal. The lighted windows were tiny in the distance now, but I still imagined his shape against them. I closed my eyes, not quite in time to prevent a tear from slipping out. His last words had been a promise to call. We'd see.

Home awaits me. The city, the traffic, my dog, Rusty, my brother, Ron, and the agency, my work, the routine.

I'm promising myself that I'll start working out, but I know it's probably just another easily broken resolution.

Charlie's Back!

Charlie returns home to Albuquerque after her Hawaiian vacation. Her brother, Ron, meets her at the airport. And guess what? Ron's in love. Is there anything worse than a middle-aged man smitten silly?

Yes — Charlie finds out, when it turns out that Ron's new sweetie is almost twenty years younger! Cute Vicky is full of secrets and Ron is about to get hurt.

In addition to Ron's problems, Charlie runs into an old friend whose business partner has apparently just committed suicide. If that's true, Sharon Ortega will probably lose her business. If it wasn't suicide, Sharon might end up in jail for murdering her partner.

It's a no-win situation until Charlie sorts out the puzzle.

Watch for the third Charlie Parker Mystery Coming in 1996.

Intrigue Press

Bringing you the finest in Mystery, Suspense, and Adventure fiction.

If your favorite bookstore doesn't carry Intrigue Press titles, ask them to order for you.

Most stores can place special orders through their wholesalers or directly with us. So, don't go without your favorite books — order today!

And if you liked this book, recommend it to your friends!

10-2-17

M   2195   954262
Shelton, Connie.
Vacations can be murder

DATE DUE			

9-96

Readers Services